Travels With Bubba

by

Gene Cate

You just hope that when the ship comes to dock, you can say, "Damn, we had a good time!"---James Jordan

one

"Wherein we are introduced
to our hero..."

Somebody wanted to know if my real name was Bubba so I guess I'd better set the record straight.

My real name is Pat Convoy but I use Bubba as a nom de plume to avoid being confused with that famous writer with the screwed up family.   I swear, one of these days they're gonna make a movie out of that boy's laundry list.   Of course, his grits aren't ground quite fine enough just like Truman, Tennessee and some of our other southern geniuses. Sadly, none of them ever wrote about food like the dear, departed Lewis who knew about grilling and deep-frying as only a true southern gourmand could. Maybe ol' Dan from Fort Worth rates a nod 'cause he knows that a hamburger is fried in grease and a chicken-fried steak is food for the gods.

I suspect that while on a book tour, Lewis was poisoned by a cabal of nutrition writers who were scared that food editors were going to wake up to the realization that about ten people read those lowfat and lite diet food features.   Then, as a little job security, they managed to plant stories about him having some kind of heart problems.   Don't food editors know that 99 44/100 percent of their readers are making millionaires out of anyone with a burger franchise? Nobody ever stood in line for a tofu-topped soy bean burger.   People want food with substance and flavor, meaning grease, salt, fat and calories. I say give'em recipes so they can clog their arteries in the privacy of their own home. I'll bet you that a double-whopper with cheese and a side order of fries will still be around when tofu is ancient history.

As usual, I tend to wander off the subject at hand which was to tell you a little about myself and a few of my friends. Anyhow, my best friend, Clyde "Z.Z." Ryder, (we call him that 'cause he slept through the entire tenth grade. Z.Z.'s pretty smart so we just figured he was bored.) and I were born and raised down here in Edsel County, Florida. Edsel is sort of a bastard stepchild of a county wedged between Dade and Monroe counties which contain Miami and the keys, respectively. It's hard to find on the map 'cause it's mostly a state of mind.

Folks occasionally ask why the county seems so distinctly southern when wedged between two cultural extremes on either side. To the north, you've got your Cubans, Haitians, New Yorkers and other foreigners and to the south, you've got about as strange a mix as ever washed up on the beach. In the keys, they think weird behavior is holding a job, paying your bills and bathing with some degree of regularity. A great egalitarian society exists with millionaire yachtsmen partying alongside a societal dropout from a mangrove thicket.

We've got our share of folks from other places but the tone of the county is pretty much set by the natives. You see, most of us are descended from refugees that came south around the end of the War of Northern Aggression. There was a goodly number of folks that chose malaria and the Seminoles over carpetbaggers or, for that matter, a firing squad; the story being that more than a few members of the Confederate army bailed out when they saw the handwriting on the wall. And they rightly guessed they'd be safe from both soldiers and Seminoles as those two managed to keep each other occupied up in the Everglades for some years. Those early settlers scratched out homesteads and took up where they'd left off before the war. Thus they went largely undisturbed until Flagler's railroad cut through the area making it accessible to the masses. Only in recent years has heavy development come to the county just like everywhere else in South Florida and now native-born Edselonians are fast becoming a minority.

Edsel County has most everything a man could ask for providing you like mosquitoes the size of robins and those damned little no-see-ums known to be the most ferocious on the North American continent. We have the agricultural richness of south Dade and the laid-back independence of the keys; not to mention the aquatic abundance afforded by our proximity to the waters of the Gulf Stream and Biscayne Bay.

Thank God, some years back, Z.Z. and I had the foresight to buy a few acres of ~~mangrove swamp~~ prime property as an investment. Not much has come of it so far but some fellow from up in Fort Lauderdale told us to hang on to it as it would make a great parking lot. He oughta know, I guess, they grow a lot of pavement up there.

All in all, I have to say that we've got it good here and we'll enjoy it as long as we can. I've got a good job at the hogwash and Z.Z. drives a long-haul truck for a living. We've got a lot of good friends and the living is still easy; but don't tell anybody. Let's keep it this way as long as possible.

two

<u>"Wherein our hero sets the tone..."</u>

My only family, (aside from Z.Z., who's like a brother) is my sister, her husband and their couple of curtain climbers. Sis and Ol' Whatsisname just bought a brand new place over in a new upscale development named Doublewide Vistas. They've got a beautiful waterfront lot overlooking the settling pond and their interior designer outdid him/herself by matching the siding on the house to the color of the pond. No small feat, that. Matter of fact, I was just over there this past weekend for a housewarming party. I'll tell you about it.

Before leaving home, I searched my wine cellar for an appropriate gift and after eliminating an '82 MD20/20 and a young but bold '88 Thunderbird; I settled on a case of '78 Billy beer. Nothing's too good for Sis and Ol' Whatsisname. Needless to say this was the hit of their cocktail party and the perfect foil for Sis's great hors d'oeuvres. She made her special Cheese Whiz and quacamole stuffed tortilla and darned if IT didn't match the house and pond too. The highlight, however, was the after-cocktails visit to the area's latest contribution to culinary ecstasy.

Yessir, Greasy George's combination tackle shop and Polynesian restaurant is about as haute as you can get. It's located just off Dirt Road-95 on Green Scum Creek; follow the quaint hand-painted signs and you'll have no trouble. Anyway, we made our 4:30PM reservation right on the dot

(Ol' Whatsisname says its unsophisticated to eat too early) and though the place was crowded, we were seated immediately with our waitress who said she was just too tired from being at the sawmill all day to stand anymore. I told everybody to order anything they wanted and it was on me. I figured if the twenty bucks I had on me wouldn't handle the tab, I could always break out the plastic from Usury Express. Hell, I was good for a hundred-dollar credit line on that sucker.

Anyway, Ol' Whatsisname said we were lucky because George always had the same special on Friday and it was his signature dish. Well, the kids weren't up to the fancy stuff so we just ordered a raccoon road pizza for them but we went for the gusto. Let me tell you, I don't remember much about the rest of the meal but the entrée was to die for.

You haven't approached gourmet nirvana until you have had Armadillo-on-the-Halfshell! I knew from the minute I laid eyes on it that this was something special. It was presented on a plastic replica of a '62 Cadillac hubcap and, in keeping with the latest trend toward the vertical look, the armadillo's tail stuck up for at least a foot. It was lightly sauced with what I later learned was a reduction of chopped okra and Gatorade. Sis said that's where the decorator got the idea for the drapes in the house. I asked the waitress how they managed to get so many armadillos each week and I think she said they used AAA Food Purveyors. I'm pretty sure that's right because I saw a sign when we got back to the main road that said "24-hour AAA service".

I was curious about the other nightly specials and Ol' Whatsisname said that it was, "...sorta catch-as-catch can. They don't know until they check the traps out back every morning."

Yessir, I've cultivated quite an interest in fine food and Edsel County is on what you call your cusp when it come to eats.

three

"Wherein the odyssey begins..."

Hot dog! I'm off to California with my old buddy, Z.Z.; he's driving cross-country now for Fen's Peat Moss Co. and asked me if I wanted to ride to the left coast with him. Seeing as how I just got laid off from my job down at the hogwash because of this "mad pig" thing, I agreed and told him that this would be a good opportunity to visit the cradle of that new-velle-cosine. Well, Z.Z. said that reminded him of Loubelle Bodine, his cousin that had a passion for food, always calling a cucumber "Darling" or a zucchini "Sugar", I decided this was better left unexplained as I knew he ate dinner over at her house every couple of weeks.

So, we're off to the land of---what did that guy call it---the Lotus Eaters? Maybe I'll get a chance to try one. A lotus, that is. Probably find one at that place...uh, can't recall the name just now but the chef's got a funny name; Hockey Puck or some such.

Z.Z. says we might stop in Nawleans, Big D and at some guy named Al B. Kirk's place. I'll log on with an update next chance I get. "10-4" (that's the way Z.Z. talks).

four

Laissez le bon temps roulez!   Miss Magnolia DuBayou taught me that. "It's a good time for rolls." is what it means. She said she works in a place called Thibodeux's Maison Du Pain, which I figured out must be a Cajun bakery.   I asked her if I could get a couple of hot baguettes there and she said, "Anything, anytime...in fact, we can go right now!"   Well, Z.Z. had wandered on down Bourbon Street while I was talking to Miss DuBayou so I told her I'd better find him before going to Thibodeux's.   To make a long story short, I couldn't find Z.Z. and Miss Magnolia was gone when I got back a little while later. I guess she figured to sell her buns on another corner.

After looking for Z.Z. for another hour or two, I was getting hungry so I started looking for this place I'd heard about called E-mail's.   Well, I wandered around for two or three hours without any luck. There were a couple of places that looked promising; you know, busy and all; but one was a navy officer's club and the other had tourists camped out in front.   One couple that I talked to had been there for three days waiting to get in.   She drove back and forth to Beaumont to feed the kids while he held their place in line.

Anyway, I wound up in what's called "the Garden District" and soon found a quaint little restaurant.   Let me tell you,

"Bistro Stud Pansy" was one great place. The maitre d' couldn't have been more helpful when I explained my travails. He said he knew Thibodeux's well and they had something for every taste. E-mail's, on the other hand, was passé and I was standing in the newest spot in town. He apologized because both tables were occupied but said I could sit at the bar if I liked. That was fine with me and a nice lady at the bar gave me one of the three stools she had been sitting on. She said her name was Babe and introduced me to her bartender friend, Butch; a little tiny thing with spikey hair and the tattoo of a Mack bulldog on her bicep. You know, like that hood ornament on the semis? I asked her if she knew Z.Z. (that's what he drives).

There wasn't a menu as they had a prix fixe special each night. I told them to bring it on. Let me say this, those California boys are going to have to tighten their toques to beat the Bistro. First, there was the salad; a bed of poached gladiola stems tossed in a catsup and bitters *vinaigre de toilette* sprinkled with grated jack cheese and acorn bits. The entrée was a chicken lips and Terrebon Parrish tadpole etoufée over Spanish moss. This was a bit of a disappointment as a couple of the tadpoles looked as if they had a little life in them yet but three or four spoonfuls of filé powder seemed to quieten them down.

The highlight of the evening was the dessert, Rhubarbs Foster! At least the one bite I had was good. Just as I was digging in, Marcel the waiter, overdid the flambé at one of the tables and caught the crepe paper drapes on fire. Well, you know how it is with those old places. Faster than you could say, "Lake Pontchartrain", the Bistro was history. I didn't even get to finish my bottle of '68 Garrison Cellars.

Well, Z.Z. made it back to the truck about noon the next day looking a little peaked. He said he had caught a case of the 24-hour "Bimbeau Flu" but might live if we could make it to Texas and get a couple of Lone Stars and chicken-fried steaks.

five

"Wherein a detour takes place..."

The main thing was we were out of New Orleans. Just in time, we got out of there before the blues festival started. Wall to wall wannabes. Never seen so many white guys in limos going to sing about hard living and hard times. Z.Z. says not a one of them knows what a "...wang, dang, doodle..." is and if their "mojo" was working, they damn sure wouldn't be. Makes sense to me...

Anyway, we made it over the Texas line and decided we would be too late for lunch and too early for dinner in Dallas, so we just kept on keeping on. Somewhere around Carlsbad, we made a wrong turn and in the wee hours of the morning found ourselves in Roswell, New Mexico. That's where we found the truck stop. Out in the middle of nowhere, this place had more strobe flashers than Studio Snort ever had. Little green lights flashed around the roof and red neon was pulsing under the aluminum skirt around the place. Some of the lights were out on the big sign which read "U____ F_____ O_____ ". As we got closer we could see that the paint read "Uncle Frank's Outpost". At this point, we didn't much care about anything but bread and water. Twenty-two hours across Texas on Pearl and pills will do that to you. So, this had to be the place.

Well, the wind must blow straight from Alamogordo to Roswell because this area had definitely seen some fallout. To start with, everybody in the place was about four feet tall and a little bug-eyed. They were pretty friendly though cause they smiled and showed a lot of teeth; about thirty-two across the front. We picked a high-top to one side and told the waitress to bring us a couple of greasewiches and a bunch of coffee cause we had some miles to go. She nodded and mumbled something that sounded like "Xwercpt unda poo.". Then she whips out a laptop and does a quick brown fox on it and quicker than you could say, "Beam us up, Scotty!", we've got plates of food in front of us.

I guess they didn't get the bugs out of the system yet. You know how it is when they first open; a waiter punches in rack of lamb and you get a slice of spam. What we got, I really can't say. I figured that the thing to do was eat it and get on the road. We did just that in spite of the fact that it looked like a combination of lime jello and two-day-old guacamole between two slices of toasted tofu about the size of a White Castle. The coffee looked like coffee but tingled your tongue like ginger ale or something. The funny thing was, everything tasted good. After the first couple of bites, we dug right in and didn't pay any more attention to the colors. We were going to order more but Z.Z. said he was full and I realized I felt the same.

We got the check and Z.Z. whipped some plastic on the waitress who promptly bit down on it like a silver dollar and handed us a receipt. It wasn't until we were pulling into LaLa Land almost 48 hours later that we realized we hadn't stopped to do anything but gas the truck since leaving Roswell. Of course, we had sung every song we ever knew going back to the "Teensy, Weensy Spider..." and told jokes when we weren't singing. Neither one of us had a wink of sleep or even felt drowsy. Z.Z. allowed as how we might just stop by there on the way back and ask for the recipe. He said their colors worked better than the blacks and reds he usually lived on between coasts.

Well, writing has made me a little sleepy so I guess I'll try to rest up for a foray onto the local food scene. Might be hard finding a good lotus blossom.

six

"Wherein our intrepid gourmands (?) discover the secrets of the Pacific rim..."

What a hoot this town is! Movie stars on every corner! Sunset Boulevard is loaded with young starlets from the movies. Z.Z. was so taken with the whole scene that he stopped one young lovely and asked her if he had seen her in "Rebecca of Silicone Farm". She said, "Naw." but that he might have seen her in "Hot Tofu Nights". Z.Z. said he didn't watch the food network too much but he'd be sure to look out for it now.

Anyway, she told me that the hottest new place in town was called D. Ray's and we ought to try it. I figured it was a franchise operation because we used to have a drive-in back home called Donnie Ray's Burger Barn and Quick-lube. She didn't think so but gave us directions and we decided to give it a shot.

Well, don't bother! Quelle disappointment! We didn't even get in the place. The maitre d, who looked like a fugitive from the men's room at the bus station, told us there was a two-year wait for a Monday night reservation. It all turned out for the best though as we learned later that the place didn't even offer food. When and if you got a table, you were served a fifty-dollar bottle of designer boutique water to hold you over while you sat there and watched the other people watch you. Those people've been breathing too much spandex or something.

I guess they don't do much home cooking out here as every place we went there were scads of people waiting to get in. Anyhow, we wound up at a place in Westwood called "Fat Thai's Pacific Pizza and Microbrewery." and before you could say, "Demi Moore's done gone and got naked again.", we were seated. There was a reason for this as we were to find out the hard way.

The pizza menu ran the gamut from A to Z, literally I mean. The triple A was alfalfa sprouts, avocado and abalone and the Z was topped with a thin layer of tofu sprinkled with squid ink to make it look about like those fake zebra-skin throw pillows you buy at the factory outlet store on the by-pass. Z.Z. thought we ought to go for something down the middle so we ordered a combo JKL and a couple of drafts. That's JKL as in jellyfish, kumquat and, you guessed it, lotus blossoms. All I can say is, "It didn't look very good but it sure did taste bad." We told the waitress that we wanted to send it back because we figured when the cook tossed the crust up it came down with an acoustic ceiling tile stuck to it. She explained that this was a rice cake crust; a Pacific rim speciality.

At this point, Z.Z. expressed his concern about the beer flavor and our helpful waitress offered to exchange it for another popular flavor. It seems we had been drinking licorice lager which was their number one seller. We allowed as how we probably wouldn't like the persimmon pale ale either. We said we'd just take a glass of water to help choke down the pizza and when she said, "Domestic or foreign?", we figured it was time to settle up and be on our way.

Now I know why it costs seven dollars to get into a movie. These movie people out here must spend a fortune on food every week. I thought the pizza was nine dollars and the extra zero was just a misprint. Wrong!!! Ninety dollars for the pizza and eighteen apiece for the beers but she agreed to scratch them off if we didn't make a fuss about the twenty-seven percent gratuity. She had to make a payment to her plastic surgeon. We agreed and bailed out of there.

When I remarked on the high cost of Pacific rim cuisine, Z.Z. muttered something about us getting "...rimmed all right." He was a little testy anyway because the company dispatcher told him that on the way home he had to take a load of fruits and nuts to Kansas City. Z.Z. told him they'd be a damned sight more comfortable on a Greyhound bus. I think I'd better get him on the open road soon; the smog is getting to him. Like, Eastward Ho!

seven

"Wherein Z.Z. subs for an ailing Bubba..."

zdPRqx..//:" now is tHe Yime for the quick lazee dog...

There we go. Hello out there. It's Z.Z. here trying to figure this thing out. Bubba's a little under the weather; says he thinks he got hold of some bad oysters; them Rocky Mountain kind. Anyway, he can't type too much between the stomach cramps and all so he said I'd better bring you up-to-date.

So, here goes. First off, we loaded up some freight for Kansas City and beat feet out of Lost Angeles. Bubba said we might as well make a little detour through Las Vegas and check out the eats there seeing as we were in the area. I allowed that leaving Sodom by the Pacific for Gomorrah in the desert wasn't much of an improvement and besides, there probably wasn't any food in Vegas that you couldn't eat with one hand while standing up.

But, I figured I'd humor him 'cause he's kind of set his mind on checking as many places as he can and writin' about them. My girlfriend, Natasha, says it has something to do with his getting kicked out of the Culinary Institute of Yeehaw Junction after his finger got caught in the pickle slicer. He called it reverse sexism 'cause they kept her on and graduated her with honors.

Anyhow, we jumped on I-15 and headed for the neon sunrise. Bubba says that when California breaks off and disappears into the ocean, Nevada is gonna have some prime oceanfront lots.

We got there a little after supper time so figured we'd clean up and hit the town. About here is when our luck turned. We had unhitched the trailer so we could take the cab to the strip and when Bubba jumped out to put some money in the meter, darned if he didn't win twenty-five dollars. Next he grabbed one of those tourist guides out of the rack and before you could say "Wayne Newton can't afford no more Danke Schön." some guy was snapping pictures and another guy was saying Bubba had just pulled out the umpty-thousandth copy and they was back-slapping and some big, tall redheaded gal was kissing him and Bubba was back-slapping her too, only a little lower and little slower. About that time, I heard something about "...everything's on us.", so I grabbed the photographer and asked him just what that meant.

"Just what it says, friend!" he answered. "You guys can eat and drink all you want, anywhere you want until sunup tomorrow! It's a big tourist promotion!"

About then I remembered what Snuffy Smith in the comics used to say: "Time's a'wastin!", so I grabbed Bubba who grabbed the redhead and we took off. Oh yeah, the redhead's name was Mitzi and she phoned her sister Ditzi and so we had a foursome. It was around midnight when we teed off.

The girls said that the El Gluteous Maximus was the place to go and we could still make the late supper show so that's where we headed. Turned out the show wasn't much; just a couple of old boys in tight pants cracking whips over some mangy mountain lions but the girls seemed to enjoy it 'cause they licked their lips a lot and went, "Woooo!" They said the two were known around those parts for their whip work. I said they couldn't hold a candle to Lash LaRue.

Hold on a minute while I ask Bubba for a few details. Things got a little hazy after the fourth or fifth bottle of Dom Cro-Magnon.

Okay, Bubba says to get on to the food, he'll tell me what to write. For an appetizer with the champagne, we had a Gila Liver Pate; this was followed by a salad of hearts of barrel cactus in agave aspic. The main course was called breast of squab en brochette with garlic-whipped rutabaga ringed with peyote mushroom buttons. (I told Bubba it wasn't nothing but roadrunner on a stick and mashed turnips but he says this way they can charge $69.95 and get away with it.) None of us much cared as long as the wine kept coming. We had chosen a '96 Twistoff Cellars blush Chablis to accompany the birds and it seemed to work just fine. Nobody retched.

Bubba says the chocolate something-or-other for dessert was fine but I didn't get any. At least I didn't eat any; it didn't look too good the next morning when I found it in my pants pocket.

He says I insisted on leaving a tip for the headwaiter, which I did. I told him, "Don't cash no checks for me toward the end of the month." That's a fact.

Anyhow, when I woke up at the crack of noon, some fool was riding a Harley hog around inside my head but we managed to get the rig hooked up and headed out of Vegas. I didn't even get a chance to tell the girls goodbye.

So, now we're stuck here outside of Denver until Bubba can go more than fifteen minutes without a pit stop.

eight

"Wherein Bubba regains his health and Z.Z. suffers a relapse of sorts..."

Thank God for Kansas City! Man cannot live by Pepto-Bismol alone. He must have a big old steak every now and then to restore body and spirit. For a couple of days there, my spirit was wondering if my body would ever see solid food again. Between Z.Z.'s mother of all hangovers and my stomach distress, the past few days have not been amongst our better times. One minute, Z.Z. was moaning about his head and the next he was complaining about his failure to consummate his brief affair with Ditzi. When I tried to explain that things had worked out for the best seeing as how Mitzi and Ditzi were transvestites, he said he didn't care where they were from or even if they were Dracula's daughters. He almost came unglued when I explained that they were brothers.

I thought I'd get his mind off it so I started talking about truck driving which is Z.Z.'s second favorite topic. I gave up though after I asked him what he'd do if the brakes went out on the rig while we were going down one of those ten-thousand-foot mountains and he said he'd make sure I was awake. When I asked him what good that would do, he said, "Not one damn bit, Bubba, but you've never seen a really

BAD wreck!" I spent the rest of the day humming the late Harry Chapin's tune, "Thirty-thousand-pounds of Bananas."

Anyhow, we made it safely down to some flat country and just outside Kansas City we found the Susan B.(as in Bull) Anthony Steak and Cigar Emporium. We figured the place had lots of class because they had valet parking for all the semis that were there. Well, we fell in line behind a couple of Kenworths and a Peterbilt and quicker than you could say, "Roger Miller's gone to that big truck stop in the sky.", a little old gal jumped up on the running board and opened my door and said, "Welcome to the Bull!" It took me a couple of seconds to realize that it was Butch, the bartender from the Bistro Stud Pansy in Nawleans. I asked her what she was doing in KC and she said that the day after the fire she rode back up here with Babe who owns the Susan B. Anthony. Well, I introduced her to Z.Z. and told her this was the fellow with the Mack truck I had asked her about at the bistro that night. Butch said to let her park the truck and she'd take a break, tell Babe that we were here and get us settled at a table. "Besides," she said, "Your boy there looks like he could use a little tune up."

As soon as Butch had parked the rig, we all went inside and she led us to a big old table in one corner of the room. It was raised up about eighteen inches and had a view of the whole place. On this platform, there was this huge chair that Butch said was Babe's "throne". We made ourselves comfortable while Butch went off to find our hostess. Pretty soon, here comes Babe, working the tables as she crossed the floor of the place. She called most everybody by name and when she got to the table she called us both by name and gave us a big hug. By the time we got our breath back, she had ordered a bottle of Old Dildo Sour Mash and set-ups. "You boys look like you could use a good meal; why don't you let me order for all of us?" That sounded like a good idea and it was, I reckon.

The appetizer of Carpaccio of Castrati Calf was followed by a Sappho Salad. Then came the main course which was a spit-roasted shoulder of plains buffalo with side orders of garlic masochist potatoes and old maid asparagus. With dessert and wine it was about the biggest meal I'd ever seen. I did the best I could to keep from offending our hostess and I figured if push came to shove, a fifth of Maalox might see me through the night. Afterwards, Babe and I had a couple of El Fidelo Gordo cigars with some brandy and I figured I was going to live after all.

Butch and Z.Z. had talked about diesels engines all through the meal and then excused themselves to see about "...Z.Z.'s injector problem". I thought the rig was running fine but Z.Z. said that Butch could probably tweak it up just a bit. All I know is, one more tune-up like that and I figured I'd be driving the rest of the way home; he looked like death warmed over the next morning. Z.Z. says he's had it with all these foreigners we keep running into on this trip. "Bubba, let's get home to Florida and see some of those good ol' snowbirds. I'm damned tired of these Transvestites and Lesbanese."

Somehow, I didn't have the heart to remind him that we had to drop a load of meat in Hotlanta right in the middle of the Olympics. This may break a good man. If he makes it home without flipping out, I'm going to paint "Marathon Man" on the doors of his truck.

nine

"Wherein our heroes go for the gold..."

A lotta years ago, Brother Dave Gardner, one of the south's more astute sages said, "...the people in south Georgia think that Herman Talmadge is God and when they die they're going to Atlanta." Well, a whole bunch of folks didn't wait to die to converge on the city. Ol' Herm is probably spinning in his grave right now 'cause he didn't make it to the t-shirt Olympics. To give the devil his due, however, even Talmadge might have been embarrassed by what Atlanta went thru in the name of international sportsmanship. It wasn't pretty.

Leaving KC, Z.Z. was like the old mule headed for the barn and he wasn't of a mind to stop until we got to Atlanta where we could unload and hit I-75 for Florida. We didn't even slow down going thru Nashville which surprised me as I figured Z.Z. would want to do a little celebrity hunt. He allowed as how the Grand Old Opry had moved from the Ryman Auditorium and all of the new crop of country stars looked like refugees from a Madonna road show except for the big hats. To protest, we drove for twenty-five miles on either side of Nashville listening to Kenny G. on some "lite jazz" station. Pepto-Bismal can't cure that bellyache!

Well, we figured that it would take all day to get across Atlanta what with all the traffic but we were in for a real surprise. Somehow, everybody was staying home; that is everybody that hadn't rented their home out for a few thousand dollars a day and gone to Hilton Head for the duration. Riiiight!! Scarlet couldn't have gotten two-hundred a day for Tara before they burned it.

We drove sixty-miles an hour right into Buckhead and quicker than you could say, "John Tesh ain't real good at that either!" we had unloaded our consignment of prime Kansas City ground water buffalo at Cafe Mogodishu on Peachtree.

I mentioned that we ought to take time to see at least one or two Olympic events and we had a chance to buy tickets to the synchronized swimming finals for fifty-cents apiece but Z.Z. was bound to get on the road. Some guy offered us two tickets at five-hundred-dollars each to see, "...young, nubile girls perform all kinds of contortions and unbelievable acts." but Z.Z. said the TV coverage of girls' gymnastics was better.

We decided that the Cafe Mogodishu wasn't for us and there was no way we were going to get into the Buckhead Bistro. Since I knew that Z.Z. was in no mood to put up with anymore strange waitrons, I said I'd just as soon get on down the road and hit some barbecue joint down around Tifton or Waycross.

We'd just left town when we heard on the radio that some fool had planted a bomb in a crowd of people at a concert in Centennial Park. Z.Z. allowed as how, "...some chickenshit sumbitch is probably mad cause Coca-Cola don't put the name of the towns on the bottom of their bottles anymore!" I left that one alone.

It turns out that one-third of the people there were athletes, coaches or others directly involved in the games, one-third were media types looking for freebies and stories and the rest were selling t-shirts. At least Lester Maddox wasn't there selling ax handles; or was he?

In Waycross, just off the highway, we found Bellbottom's BBQ and Brake Service. We grabbed a couple of stools and ordered a pitcher of good old sweetened iced tea from the waitress. She said her name was Willie Mae and she and her husband ran the place. She called him "The Chief" 'cause he'd previously been a navy cook for about thirty years. Well, we had some goat ribs and baked garbanzos which was just fine and then Willie Mae offered us some cookies and coffee for dessert. She said they were "The Chief's" personal creation and, in fact, he had just finished this batch. Z.Z. said we'd pass 'cause he'd seen "The Chief" rolling out the balls of dough and then slapping them in his belly button to make the little swirl on top. Willie Mae said, "That's nothing. You oughta see him make doughnuts." We settled for a slice of Vidalia onion pie and hit the road for the last leg home.

We were heading downhill now and nothing short of the good lord was going to stop us.

ten

"Wherein it's hard to come home after a long month..."

You didn't expect to get off that easy, did you? Naw. We crossed that old Florida line and Z.Z. let out a whoop and said, "We're almost home, Bubba. I hope Natasha Sue has got the hot tub fired up 'cause I'm gonna dive in that thing and stay till I shrivel up like a prune." I allowed as how

Natasha might not appreciate him being too shriveled up but he just giggled and mumbled something about her learning in HomeEc how to reconstitute dried fruit.

I have to admit it did feel good to be back in the Sunshine State although that's not quite accurate 'cause you might as well be in south Georgia until you hit Ocala and that's just a misplaced part of Kentucky what with all the thoroughbred farms. Then you come to "Let's Take a Second Mortgage On the House and Take the Kids to See the Mouse World." I'm waiting for the sinkhole of the century to swallow that whole foreign country up. I'd pay to see that.

Well, quicker than you could say, "Son, drink your OJ so you can grow up strong and beat your wife.", we had passed Yeehaw Junction and come up on the I-95 interchange. Z.Z. said he was going to get on "Insane-95" for the rest of the run; not so much to save the turnpike tolls but to watch the show.

"Bubba, between Fort Pierce and Homestead, I can guarantee you at least one shooting, two semis turned over on one side or the other; an eight-passenger van that rolled about five times and scattered thirty-four migrant workers for a half-mile; enough furniture to furnish a three-bedroom house and two women and one man nekkid as jaybirds who, with luck, will be together in the same car and you won't be able to tell who's driving. Oh yeah; I forgot...and somehow in the midst of the mayhem; just one trooper who'll be giving some dork a ticket for being by hisself in the carpool lane."

I figured I was in for my own personal "E-ticket" ride and I was right. It was just about as Z.Z. said, give or take three or four naked people.

Well, we ran out of big road and hit the three-lane suicide strip south of Florida City which told me we were nearly home. There's something mighty comforting about being able to see salt water on both sides of you. I told Z.Z. to drop me at Katie's Conch House and Radiator Repair 'cause I needed a dose of home cooking.

Z.Z pulled off onto the crushed gravel lot at Katie's, gave me a high five and said that he'd had more fun on this trip than any he could remember; at least what parts of it he could remember.

Katie's was busy but I managed to ease around the corner of the bar and find a stool. She looked up, saw me and grinned with both teeth which is pretty much it by way of a greeting in Katie's book. She pulled a Manatee Malt from the cooler, popped the top off and said it was on the house to celebrate my return. When I commented on how good business was she said, "Ever since some writer feller was in here and wrote about the 'Bouillabaisse Terre e Mer', we been swamped."

Knowing Katie's husband, Sergeant Major, worked the back of the house, my curiosity got the better of me and I inquired about the makeup of this culinary delight. (I should mention that Sergeant Major's name is derived from a small fish that abounds in the keys. They have very prominent stripes on their bodies which approximate those worn by Katie's husband during his early years on prison road gangs. Thus his name and degree from C.I.I., Culinary (Correctional) Institute of Immokalee, an Everglades prison camp.)

"Bubba, it's the same old land crab and barracuda stew you've been eating for years with a couple of gumbo limbo leaves for a garnish. The difference is now we can charge seven-fifty instead of seventy-five cents for a bowl. At the rate we're going, we'll probably need a maitre'd by Christmas and you'd be just the feller to help us out. Think about it. We already leased out the valet parking concession for three-thousand a month."

I told Katie I'd think about it but I knew that this was another case of success spoiling a fine establishment. No longer could I sit at the bar and enjoy a quiet repast of keys cuisine. The hordes had breached the gates and soon I would read about Katie and the Major in slick magazines that praised their vision of the new conch cuisine. This, and the trip around the country would put an end to my gourmet career. Food just wasn't so much fun anymore. The Manatee Malt tasted sour in my throat and it was time to go home. It was the first time I'd ever left Katie's hungry.

eleven

"Wherein our hero falls under the influence of grape and the opposite gender..."

Sometimes Lady Luck just looks down and says, "I'm gonna lay a little loving on that boy!" Well, she did that to me. Yours truly has been to the left coast again, this time as the guest of the Nubbin Ridge Winery. Some time before, I had filled out a card I found in one of the food magazines where you submit your favorite recipe and doggone if I didn't win an all-expense trip for two to Shake Francisco and a limo cruise through the wine country. My resolve to avoid further disappointing culinary experiences was offset by circumstances that occurred when the word got out around the county.

Needless to say, Z.Z. was a little upset when I told him he couldn't go with me. He calmed down though when I explained to him that when it came down to a choice between him and Candy Crawford Jr. (Edsel County's "Miss Cantaloupe of 1999") it was a no-brainer. Z.Z. agreed that, in the crunch, a 38-double-D outweighed a 35-year friendship.

What happened was, when Candy Jr. found out about me winning the trip, she became a lot more sociable when I dropped my clothes off at CeeCee's Laundromat and Elvis Memorial Aerobics Center. She brought it up for three weeks running and even said she'd always thought I was real cute for a baldheaded guy twice her age. I figured I'd better not mention how much her mother had liked my eighteen-year-old curly locks the night of the senior prom; so much so that she had almost pulled some of them out in a severe fit of like in the back seat of my car. That little secret was safe since her mother, Candy Sr., had departed this mortal coil due to a severe case of coitus interruptus brought on by four shots from a .357 magnum fired by the wife of her then partner-in-passion. Sorry, didn't mean to go off on a tangent there.

Anyhow, we arrived in San Fran and sure enough there was this limo driver waiting for us right at the airport. His name was Guido and he had about a size 19 neck and probably a size 5 hat. Well, quicker than you could say, "Ernest and Julio got purple feet.", we were loaded and on our way to the valley. Candy Jr. rummaged around in the parlor of the limo and came up with some of Nubbin Ridge's best sparkling wine called "Chilly Goose". She hollered to Guido about how long the trip would take and when he said about an hour and a half, she said, "That's just about right for two bottles of bubbly and some heavy fooling around." Well, we had the two bottles all right and some of the other too which I won't go into right here.

Soon we arrived at the winery although there was one time that was a little touchy. Candy Jr. decided that a tour bus full of wine writers needed a little inspiration so she shucked her top and stood up through the sunroof of the limo as we passed them. That's when Guido drove off the road into somebody's orchard, but using skills he said he had learned in Sicily, he managed to dodge the trees and get us safely back onto the highway. Candy Jr. allowed as how those old boys would be writing tonight about full-bodied, chewy wines with a slight essence of melon. I decided right then that there was a god and he liked me very much.

The Nubbin Ridge Winery is a very laid-back operation which is probably why they only produce about two-hundred cases of their top seller a year. The quaint reception center is a WWII-surplus quonset hut restored to its original state after being moved to abut the converted blimp hangar which serves as the winery's nerve center.

We were met by Nubbin Ridge's head vintner, Moshe Abramowicz, and given the grand tour. Turns out Moshe's a southern Baptist and provides most of the grape juice for the member churches' communions. (His brother Abie makes the communion wafers in his bagel bakery.) Anyhow, Moshe walked us through the whole process from the picking of the grapes to the final bottling and shipping. He even shared the secret of what gives their most popular red, the Dago Blush Burgundy, its unique flavor. Yessir! They age it in these old barrels (They're really nail kegs 'cause I saw on one where it said--10pX50--. That means fifty pounds of ten-penny nails.) for as long as five days. After that, they bottle and cap it and seal it up with authentic candle wax scrapings taken from old straw-covered chianti bottles from San Francisco coffee houses. I mean, these people CARE! He said we'd get to drink all we wanted at dinner with Al Fresco.

After a nap(?!) at the quaint Nubbin Ridge Inn and a little first aid on the rope burns, Candy Jr. and I were both famished so we went looking for Al Fresco's. What a spread! We had cold abalone legs with mesclun, haunch of Half Moon Bay sea lion with kelp pesto and macadamia tofu torte. I guess ol' Al was too modest to come out and accept the accolades of the dinner crowd 'cause we never did see him but he sure put on a spread. Candy Jr. was disappointed in the wine however; she said it wasn't a whole lot better than the grape Kool-Aid in the high school lunchroom. She drank just enough to get her energy up and then dragged me back to the four-poster. I told her to forget the ropes; I wasn't going anywhere.

The next three days were pretty much the same. Guido didn't have any more trouble after he took off the rear view mirror and covered the partition between the front and back. Yessir, that Candy Jr. can be a distraction.

Anyhow, we made it back home and now Z.Z. won't shut up about the fifteen pounds I lost during the trip. He says I've got to get my strength back 'cause he's got a little surprise in store. I'll bet he stops ragging me when he finds out I've got free dry cleaning for life. I earned it!

twelve

"Wherein our hero discovers that gator hunting is a crock..."

Greetings from Our Lady of Lifetime Monthly Installments Hospital; Edsel County's answer to the Mayo Clinic. I've been here for a couple of weeks now and they tell me that I'll probably get to go home in a few more days. It'll be some time though before I get rid of the pins and the cast. But, I'm getting ahead of the story.

When I got back from the wine country and Z.Z. broke the news about winning a highly-prized gator hunting license in the annual drawing put on by the state, I figured that something had fried his brain. It seems that a few months back, he'd filled out the form and submitted it without telling anybody. Of course, the state, in its infinite wisdom, chose him to be one of the nearly two-hundred fools that would be allowed to go out in the swamps and... CATCH AN ALLIGATOR. Not only did he pay a pile a money for the license, go to a class put on by the state, buy a harpoon, a grappling hook and a bang stick; he bought another license naming me his assistant. I told him that the closest I was gonna get to an alligator was when I went into my closet and passed my daddy's old alligator belt hanging there.

He reminded me that I owed him for taking Candy Jr. to California instead of him so I softened and let that idiot talk me into it. He said some people got twelve or fifteen gators and, at maybe three or four hundred dollars a hide, that was good money. Not to mention selling the tail meat. He added that he had already figured out a good place to start our hunt but he wouldn't share that knowledge until September 1st, the day the hunt started. I never learn.

Well, I did a little reading up on the subject and it seemed reasonable that two grown men, properly equipped, might just have a chance at bagging a couple of the critters. I never learn.

Z.Z.'s plan was simple, on the face of it. Edsel County Country Club's golf course, known locally as "Yucca Flats", had only one hole on the entire course that had a water hazard. This was the par-three thirteenth hole and the hazard was a pond about seventy-five yards long that started halfway down the fairway and ended up at the front of the green. For as long as anyone could remember, this pond had been home to Ol' Bogey, a very large and rather lethargic gator. Ol' Bogey could usually be seen sunning himself on the side of the pond away from the cart path although sometimes he would be floating motionless down in front of the green. The two big eyes and big snout could be a little unnerving to the transient golfer trying to save par, especially when a betting opponent would casually mention that Ol' Bogey hadn't attacked anybody in at least a month.

Z.Z.'s plan was to hook Ol' Bogey. When I allowed that this was somewhat akin to shooting fish in a barrel, Z.Z. informed me that we would be performing a public service by getting rid of him. It seems several female club members suspected their husbands of currying favor with the old bull gator by feeding the wives' yapping poodles and lazy apsos to him, thereby killing two birds with one stone. "There's no telling how many marriages we'll save." he rationalized. I never learn.

On the appointed evening around oh-dark-thirty, we loaded Z.Z.'s old flat bottomed skiff into his pickup and headed out. We parked behind the maintenance shack back of number twelve green and walked the skiff over to the pond. It took three trips to carry the boat, the hunting gear, the lights and the turkey. Yeah, the turkey; a fifteen-pound, self-basting butterball that Z.Z. had stuffed with a helium-filled condom to make sure it would float. With a piece of string tied to one of the turkey's legs, he figured we'd drag it around the pond once or twice till Ol' Bogey got a whiff of it and came for his midnight snack. Z.Z. said he'd keep the spotlight on the bird so we could see Ol' Bogey's eyes when he comes to get it.

"When he's close enough, Bubba, you nail him with the harpoon then we'll let him tow us around the pond until he gets tired. That's when I'll pop him right behind the head with the bang stick and we've got ourselves a truckload of gator." I never learn.

Do you have any idea how stupid it feels to sit in a boat in the middle of the night, in the middle of a golf course, trolling a turkey?

We'd been at it for about thirty minutes when I heard Z.Z. take a sharp breath. "Good God," he said, "Look at that!" "That" was two big eyes that, in the spotlight, looked like two red-hot charcoal briquettes floating on the water about a foot apart. Ol' Bogey eased up to the turkey and Z.Z. started pulling the line real slow to get him within range. Z.Z. whispered for me to get ready to strike him and I had a sudden premonition that this probably wasn't a good idea. Just then, Ol' Bogey opened his huge jaws and sort of inhaled the turkey. Without even thinking about it, I lunged with the harpoon and nailed him.

Quicker than you could say, "Where's Johnny Weismuller when you need him?" the big gator thrashed, rolled over a couple of times and headed for the bottom. Unfortunately, I had placed my foot in the coil of line in the bottom of the boat and he yanked me over the side breaking my leg and foot in three or four places as I went. Meanwhile, Z.Z., in an attempt to steady himself, jammed the .44-magnum bang stick against the bottom of the boat, firing it and making a rather large hole.

Now picture this: I'm snarled in the middle of a line on one end of which is the Godzilla of gators heading for parts unknown and on the other end of which is Z.Z. in the rapidly sinking skiff. My ineptness with the harpoon had its rewards, however, because soon I felt the line go slack and I was floating free. The spear had pulled loose from the old gator's hide. Finding myself in shallow water, I was able to untangle the line just as the skiff sank to the bottom of the pond. With some effort, I managed to crawl up to the cart path.

Pretty soon, Z.Z. came up the bank bitchin' about losing all the gear and how he'd have to dodge the duffers tomorrow to retrieve everything during daylight. After calling him several kinds of low-life scum, I passed out.

So, here I am being cared for by the sisters of the Order of the Inquisition and subsisting on smuggled-in pizza and burgers 'cause I won't even go into what they fed me here the first couple of days. At least it wasn't gator tail.

Well, it's about time for Candy Jr. to show up for my special therapy (there's an upside to every misfortune), so until next time...STAT!

thirteen

"Wherein Bubba is on the mend...sorta..."

Poor ol' Bubba; if it's not one thing it's another. There he is lying in the hospital with a broken leg and now he's done gone and got a broken heart.

He'd gotten over being p.o.'d at me since I was keeping him in pizza, conch burgers and Manatee Malt after the sisters tried to poison him with that hospital food. He says it's because they're mad at him on account of Candy Jr. tried to join up with them when she heard the sisters all had habits. Her twisted logic was that the hospital was giving away recreational pharmaceuticals and she wanted a piece of the action.

Anyhow, things were going pretty good for all concerned. At least Bubba was being reasonable and didn't call me seven kinds of sumbitch every time he laid eyes on me. This was a definite improvement over his first couple of days in the hospital.

The sheriff said he'd forget about the gator incident if I promised to turn in my license and keep Ol' Bogey in turkeys for ninety days. The country club allowed as how they wouldn't press charges but told us we were blackballed for life plus a few years; which didn't exactly rate as one of life's great tragedies.

The upshot was; suddenly, I was feeding a family of three: me, Bubba and Ol' Bogey.

I'll have to say that for a while Candy Jr. was doing her part to lift Bubba's spirits. She visited him every day after work and he was of a much better disposition after her visits. The only low point came when Bubba's first roommate (he had a semi-private room) croaked one night during Candy's visit. The doctors were at a loss to explain it 'cause the old man had been making good progress since his heart attack.

Well, a few days ago, Candy Jr. didn't show up for Bubba's therapy and when I brought him his supper from Katie's, he wasn't a happy picnicker. Word was that Candy Jr. had all of a sudden run off with Juan Carlos Bono, a shoe salesman from down at the Pic'n Shoes. Thank god Bubba's leg was tied to the ceiling of that room or he would have been changing that boy's name to Juanita.

As it turns out, when Bubba landed in the hospital, Candy Jr. decided that a new pair of 6" spike heels would be just the thing to cheer him up and maybe give her a little extra leverage. At the shoe store, it didn't take long for J.C. to convince Candy Jr. that he was descended from Incan royalty and had rights to the ancestral castle in Machu Picchu where she would make a pretty good queen. While he was at it, he told her it would probably be a good idea if she wasn't a virgin thereby avoiding any hungry volcanoes in the area. So, a few days later, Candy Jr. dropped the keys to her shop at her cousin's; dropped Bubba without a word and, true to her belief that you're a born-again virgin every Monday morning, dropped her drawers in the back of J.C.'s '72 Thunderbird low-rider. Last we heard, they were camped out under an I-95 overpass up in Miami waiting for the Peruvian consulate to set up a coronation.

I used to think that ladies should be treated like ladies and sluts should be idolized but after what Roboslut did to my best buddy, I may have to rethink that little pearl of wisdom.

I'll tell you one thing, all this sure makes me appreciate my main squeeze, Natasha, that much more. That sweet thing's as straight as six o'clock and no slouch in the looks department either. For someone who never had a date all through high-school, she sure has blossomed. It's amazin' what a couple of capped teeth, some contact lenses, a little strategically placed silicone and a touch-up on the roots can do. Some guys are fussy about when the drapes don't match the rug but what difference does it make in the dark?

Anyhow, Bubba asked me to stop by his house and bring him his old guitar so I figured he's gonna get a little revenge on the sisters. If you ever heard him play, you know what I mean. Let's just say he ain't no Les Paul. More like Van Halen played backward at half speed. But as long as it keeps his mind off Little Miss Mattress-back, I guess it's a good thing.

Well, I'd better go feed Ol' Bogey before I pick up the guitar then stop at Katie's for Bubba's supper. He says he'll never eat another conch burger after this but right now they'll do. I promised him I'd fix a big pot of my possum chili for his first day home. He said he couldn't wait.

fourteen

"Wherein recovery is effected and our hero finds a new vocation..."

When it comes down to a contest between my brain and my glands, the brain doesn't even make the quarterfinals. One of my dear, departed ex-girlfriends once told me, "Bubba, every time you unzip your pants, your brain falls out." Of course, that was a couple of years after she had declared undying love for my "braininess". For once, I guess I'd have to agree with her about something. But it is amazing what a twenty-three-year-old aerobics instructor can do when she puts her mind to it. Who besides Candy Jr. could have come up with "Ten Creative Uses For Ice Cubes and Ben-Gay on a Sunday Morning".

Well, that's behind me now and the last I heard her and ol'Inca-Dinky-Doo were hitching their way across Quintana Roo heading for the Andes. I wish her well in her quest for royalty and hope she doesn't run up on those Sardine rebels on the way.

Speaking of royalty (Can this boy do a segue or what?),it looks like I'm gonna get me some of the financial kind. Royalties, that is. Hold on. As usual, I'm getting ahead of myself.

The way it happened was like this: there's not a whole lot to do when you're hanging by one leg from a hospital ceiling.

After about two days of Maury, Montel, Sally and the rest; just about the time Geraldo starts to look intellectual, it's time to give the TV a rest.

Anyhow, Z.Z. brought me my guitar and I started playing around with some words that had been going thru my head. I could play probably three chords but I figured that even Chet Atkins had to start somewhere. Z.Z. used to claim that those three chords were C, H-sharp and a Q-major augmented but he's shut up now since he's trying to figure out,"...how the hell anybody that can't play *or* sing can write a hit song?"

You see, that's what I did. Yep, by the time the hospital let me go I had finished two or three songs.

Well, I sent one off to my old buddy, Zamfir Potts, who plays nose flute in the pit band at the T&A Lounge in Yeehaw Junction. Zamfir's cousin Omar is country music star Billy Ray Muckenfuss's aide-de-camp and flunky du jour. (That's a fancy title for the custodian of exotic pharmaceuticals and whip-out cash.)

Anyhow, Zamfir added about a chord and a half and sent it on to Omar who in turn showed it to the great Billy Ray. Now Billy Ray is known to have flashes of genius and inspiration after his usual breakfast of a dozen black beauties and a quart of Cuervo Gold. Such was the case on this fateful day and Billy Ray decided then and there to lead off his new album with my song. The rest, as they say, is history.

Before you could say, "Dolly's really Porter in drag...or is that the other way around?" I was on my way to Nashville to sign a contract and watch the recording session.

Now there was a train wreck. A recording session is about the closest thing I've ever seen to two horny armadillos trying a menage a trois with a bowling ball. Like they say, it seemed like a good idea.

This gang-bang started around midnight when Billy Ray, his wife Rose, his girlfriend Veronica, Omar and me showed up at Fat-Butt Falwell's Recording Studio and Gun Shop. Everybody else, meaning about fifty musicians, singers, technicians, caterers, pimps, pushers and god knows whatever was ready and raring to go. At least, the three or four that were awake seemed eager. Turns out, they'd been there for two days without a break laying down some rhythm tracks and such.

By about three in the A.M., Fat-Butt and Omar had kicked enough people awake to get started. They propped Billy Ray up in this little glass booth (by this time he was having a little trouble walking and talking) and put one of the back-up singers in there with him; to turn the pages, I guess. You couldn't see her but Billy Ray looked happy with the arrangement.

Well, if I hadn't seen it myself, I would never have believed that Billy Ray could lay down three cuts in about twenty minutes. The man is a stone genius. They called for a little break about then and Billy Ray told Omar to give the back-up girl a bonus hundred. Fat-Butt told Omar to make it two 'cause on the last cut Billy Ray had hit and held a high note that would cause dogs that heard it to run in circles and whimper. Fat-Butt told me later that Billy Ray had reached his "rectal octave". It was all too technical for me.

fifteen

"Wherein fame and fortune befall our hero..."

Special to the Edsel County Clarion
By Natasha Sue Rigsbee

...NASHVILLE...Billy Ray Muckenfuss, country music's artist of the year, has announced the release of his new album "Songs my Daddy Would've Loved To Sing In the Outhouse" featuring a tune by Edsel County's own Pat "Bubba" Convoy. Convoy's song "She was Just As Much Fun On Her Feet" was described by Muckenfuss as, "....a sad tale of lost love written by one who had to live it to tell it." The singer added that his record company expected to release a single of Convoy's tune backed by one of Muckenfuss's own entitled "Your Husband and My Wife Won't Be Home Tonight."

When asked about reports that his song was indeed based on recent events in the writer's life, Convoy's enigmatic reply was, "All life is fiction and we are but minor characters in the writer's mind." Convoy reportedly wrote the song during his convalescence from a recent hunting accident. His longtime friend, Clyde "Z.Z." Ryder, likewise refused to confirm or deny the source of the writer's inspiration saying only that, "Bubba's muse is his own business. Besides, her name wasn't Sue."

Other songs on the record, which should be in Edsel County stores soon, include "Move Over, Darling. My Wife Just Got Home" and "She's Grinding Her Grits At Another Man's Mill".

Editors note:
The Clarion was able to obtain the words to Convoy's song from Buzzard's Roost Records. Here is the entire text as recorded by Billy Ray Muckenfuss:

Let me tell you a story 'bout a girl I knew;
she was real good lookin' and her name was Sue.
When we made love, she was oh so sweet,
but she was just as much fun on her feet.

(chorus)
Yeah, she was just as much fun on her feet;
she was just as much fun on her feet.
I will boast from coast to coast
that she was just as much fun on her feet.

Well, we made love all over this town.
Yeah we spent a lot of time just fooling around.
But I loved her as much walking down the street
'cause she was just as much fun on her feet.

(chorus)
Yeah she was just as much fun on her feet;
she was just as much fun on her feet.
Lying in bed or standing on her head;
she was just as much fun on her feet.

One day Sue told me the sad, sad news;
she'd fallen for a guy that was selling shoes.
She told me ol' John just couldn't be beat
'cause he's been taking good care of her feet.

(chorus)
Oh he was having lots of fun with her feet.
Yeah he was having more fun with her feet.
Goodness knows, they were nose to toes;
but she was just as much fun on her feet

sixteen

"Wherein our hero returns in triumph...sorta..."

Don't talk too loud, please. I'm just lying up here on the porch trying not to think about music, people, booze and Nashville. I've been home for two days now and I'll probably be able to stand up long enough to brush my teeth by tomorrow.

After a fast start in the studio, things just sorta went to hell in a hand basket. Billy Ray went face down in the mixing board while we were listening to the first playbacks and despite the best efforts of Rose, Veronica and Fatbutt, stayed there for the better part of the day. What went on in the meantime is not for consumption by normal, well-adjusted Homo-sapiens that don't know the meaning of the term menage-a-group-grope.

Somehow I wound up alone with Veronica in an entanglement that lasted the better part of twelve hours and involved beer, booze, assorted medications and ointments and a bucket of fried chicken. Too late, I recalled that someone had referred to her as Veronica Velcro because, once attached, she held on pretty good.

Fortunately, Fatbutt managed to get me to the airport in time for my flight home; most of which I missed in my Nashville-induced coma. I woke up just as the plane was making a low pass over the main runway at Edsel County International Airport and Fairgrounds.

The low pass was necessary to scare off the assorted livestock that inhabited the adjacent, unfenced pasture which also doubled as long-term parking. You haven't seen a real mess until you've seen a heifer sucked through the engine of a 737; not a pretty sight.

Nor was I, for that matter. Z.Z. met me and when he saw me his only comment was, "Jesus, Bubba, every time you go out of town without me, you come back looking like death warmed over. Who was she this time?" Realizing that I was not capable of intelligent conversation, he just rattled on, bringing me up to date on happenings around the county.

It seems that Candy Jr. decided that being royalty didn't count for much if it didn't involve fancy cars, jeweled crowns and a standing army. Her cousin had reported that Juan had taken the maitre'd's job at Katie's Conch House and was gouging the customers for fifty bucks to avoid the standard two-hour wait for a table. The latest sighting of Candy Jr. had been at a topless car wash up in Hallendale which was also doing a rather brisk business.

Things had slowed down in the peat moss business so Z.Z. was subcontracting the rig to keep up his cash flow.

"Bubba, if I get that contract from the Turkey Point nuclear power plant to haul that spent fuel up to South Carolina, I'll be set for months."

He then proceeded to tell me how the AEC's Savannah River Plant outside of Aiken, SC was where the stuff was stored when it was no longer effective as fuel but could still melt your toenails for about the next two-thousand years. According to Z.Z., other than running over the occasional environmentalist freak who threw themselves under the wheels of arriving trucks, there was nothing to worry about.

"They pack it in these metal canisters and all so it's real safe and I figure if you painted 'em green and stenciled 'fresh

Florida broccoli' on each one, who's to know? Nobody ever sacrificed hisself for broccoli."

Somewhere in the nether regions of my brain, a small voice was repeating, "gator hunt...gator hunt...", but it didn't really register with me. Nor did the fact that broccoli is grown in California seem real important.

"So anyhow Bubba, I should hear from them by the first of the week and we'll take a little run up to Geecheeland." I moaned and Z.Z. tried to console me. "Poor ol' Bubba, you'll be all right in a little bit. I got two six-packs of Manatee Malt on ice and a big pot of possum chili on the stove. It'll make a new man outta you." Somehow Nashville didn't seem so bad after all.

seventeen

"Wherein another bad idea only gets worse..."

I've decided to do some research into early Anglo-Saxon law to determine if there is a precedent for getting a divorce or at least a legal separation from an old friend. I use the term advisedly. I'd settle for a court order barring Z.Z. from talking to me or coming within a hundred yards or some such.

You'd think after thirty-five or so years, I'd learn to say, "No thank you!" to any suggestion or plan that he suggests. Of course, it's not like he's talking rock-climbing, bungee jumping, nude skydiving or other perilous pursuits. I mean, I've been in the woods with him when he was was armed and there's no more careful or conscientious hunter around. But, I swear that boy could turn a walk around the block into a calamitous adventure.

When Z.Z. uses the terms, "We'll just..." or "It's only...", it's time to get the hell outta Dodge City. The simpler he makes things seem, the more likely they are to end in disaster.

Case in point: the geniuses over at Turkey Point did offer Z.Z. some exorbitant amount of money to transport the spent nuclear fuel up to South Carolina. When he found out that the cargo consisted of only a half-dozen metal drums, the plot thickened.

"Bubba, we'll rent us a Winnebago, stash the drums in the back, hire a couple of those fanny-flossing bathing suit models from up at South Beach as stewardesses and the anti-nukes won't have a clue. We'll be in and out so fast we won't even smell 'em".

I have to give the old boy credit here. Of course it doesn't take long to audition a couple of "models" when you have two cases of vintage bubbly and about fifty pounds of fresh stone crab claws to offer right up front. Anyhow, after about two hours of trolling South Ocean Drive on Miami Beach, we had signed Astrud and Gunilla on for the trip and after establishing that they were, in fact, real live girls, we were on our way.

Mistake number one: I started out driving. Now all of you are already familiar with Z.Z.'s failings as regards women and champagne; I never learn.

By the time we cleared that asphalt and concrete swamp known as Broward and Palm Beach counties, we were into the fortieth replay of "You Can Leave Your Hat On..." Good thing it was, too...; that's all anybody had on.

Somehow, I had been stripped of a pair of Topsiders, my Calvin's and one of Ralph's button-downs, not to mention a fresh pair of new Peewee Herman easy-access briefs. My wardrobe at this point consisted of a seat belt, shoulder harness and a baseball cap from Valujet Airlines. How's that for a harbinger of doom?

Fortunately, most of the drivers on Idiot-95 missed the spectacle of Astrud and Gunilla doing pressed hams against the picture window in the side of the camper. But some kid that was videotaping telephone poles is going to be a hero with his buddies because, just before dark, we spent about five minutes right alongside him while the girls did some u-turns.

By this time, we were just crossing the Georgia line and the welcome station seemed a reasonable place to stop and rest a bit. We didn't want to get to the plant too early anyway so we eased over in the back lot next to the semis sorta out of sight of any impressionable children that might be about.

You remember Barbara and Louise singing about how some guy could eat crackers in their bed anytime? Let me tell you, crackers are baby powder compared to a pile of shells from a mess of stone crab claws. I woke up about four in the A.M. thinking I was the swami guy in the carnival that slept on a bed of nails. Apparently, we had used the master bed of the camper as a dining table and I had not been able to navigate elsewhere after what I hoped had been dinner. Tiny bits of broken shell were imbedded in my back and I could only be grateful that I hadn't rolled over during the night.

What I presumed to be Z.Z. and either Gunilla or Astrud were on the floor covered by two or three blankets. Actually, I could see enough of Z.Z.'s face to recognize him although about half of it was covered by one or the other girl's foot.

I stumbled toward the camper's bathroom leaving a trail of broken shells in my wake only to find the other girl asleep in the tiny shower. She was wearing my Peewee underwear and a Mayflower Van Lines cap. Don't ask, don't tell.

Somehow, in the debris, I managed to make a pot of coffee, find a pair of jeans and a sweatshirt and get the show on the road. By this time, Gunilla, (the one from the shower) was semi-coherent and was nuking some frozen burritos for breakfast. Suddenly, I developed a craving for some possum chili. Z.Z. and Astrud hadn't moved and some little devil inside me was sorta wishing he was dead. We were still on the uphill side of this trip and I knew we were in for a long climb.

eighteen

"Wherein a danse macabre takes place..."

You know that old saying, "You can't get there from here. You have to go some place else to start?" Well, that's what you have to do to get to that Savannah River nuke place. We crossed into South Carolina on I-95 and then had to start all over again. Lewis and Clark would have gotten lost trying to read the map and navigate the back roads between Ridgeland and Aiken. Fortunately, we finally found some signs directing us to the main gate of the place and, sure enough, with Z.Z. driving, we managed to play the lost tourist game right up to the entrance. Z.Z. remarked that the few protesters we saw on the way in were a good argument for either abortion or the atom bomb. Nobody touched that one.

The gate guards were a little skeptical of the Winnebago until the girls invited one of them inside to guide us to the drop-off point. Picture this: Astrud and Gunilla were dressed in white Spandex coveralls at least two sizes too small with the dangerous radiation symbol over the left breast and a logo bearing the inscription "(B)ubba's (I)nterstate (T)ransport (E)nterprise" over the right. I never said Z.Z. was stupid, just dangerous.

Anyhow, quicker than you could spell "Chernobyl" we had unloaded the goods and the guard who, by this time, was suffering from fallout which is what happened every time one of the girls bent over. Before making our break from ground zero, we did learn that there were big doings over in one of the neighboring towns so we decided to check it out.

The town of Salley, South Carolina was just a hop, skip and a couple of dead possums from where we were so we decided to check out the annual festival there known as the "Chittlin' Strut". (This is where a scholar would normally insert a footnote to explain a term that may not be familiar to your average reader. However, if you gotten this far is this saga, you grew up knowing that a chittlin', AKA chitterling, is a hog intestine that has been scrubbed, rinsed, boiled, fried and/or been through other numerous processes to make it edible(?). That's right, folks. The chittlin' is a southern delicacy. You Yankees can thank your stars that you won the war or you would be eating them right now in some fancy joint on New York's upper East Side. Unfortunately, we lost the conflict so the chittlin' is not a major export.)

Anyhow, we were fortunate enough to approach the town from upwind and park the Winnebago on the main drag just before the parade started. Soon, here comes the fire truck, the police chief or, in this case, the entire one-man force, the seven-piece high school marching band and the Strut Queen, Miss RuPaul Rodman, who was the star of the girls' basketball team.

Now we're talking twelve thousand visitors starving for a taste of chittlins' in a town with an average population of about 98.6 people. To put it mildly, the infrastructure was overloaded. The line from the girls' Port-a-let stretched into the adjoining county and the smart girls used the boys' potty cause they knew boys don't use those things. Like dogs, they just seek out the nearest tree or other stationary, vertical object.

Z.Z. volunteered to brave the food line and return with the requisite chittlin' dinners accompanied by french fries, slaw, rolls and whatever else came in the styrofoam du jour. The girls offered to go with him and I seconded the motion as I figured this was a chance to catch a nap that might be the difference between overdose and death.

Two hours later, waking up alone and hungry, my first thought was to wonder what could be taking so long. This was instantly replaced by the knowledge that all was not well and would surely get worse before it was over. I was learning.

Sure enough, the inevitable knock on the door came within minutes and there was the police force...er...chief.

"You Bubba Convoy?"

"Yessir."

"You know a feller name of Clyde? Says you're from some book of world records and you can explain what he was doing in the high school auditorium with two half-nekkid wimmen."

"What exactly was he doing?" I didn't think I wanted to hear the answer.

"Well, you see, we have a good ol' boy name of Elroy who dances the Strut for us every year and he's been on national TV and all that but he kinda got sidetracked when these two girls in some kinda Martian outfits showed up. Anyhow, the girls started doing something they called the Macaroni and next thing we know, he's lost the Strut and gone into some kinda St. Vitus' dance. All of a sudden, here comes the Strut queen and that fella Clyde looking like they're melted together. Well, the crowd's loving it but Preacher Kinney, who doubles as mayor, didn't like it. When he tried to stop it, the Queen grabbed him and wrapped around him like the serpent in the garden. The two Martians did the same with your friend and Elroy and they won't stop. Says when you certify them for the Macaroni record, they'll stop."

It was clear to me that someone was confusing the Macarena with the Lambada.

Some hours later, reflecting on the fact that I had had the keys to the camper and a clear shot out of town, I reckoned my loyalty to Z.Z. could no longer be questioned. Instead of making my break, I had accompanied the gendarme back to the auditorium, extricated my wastrel friend from the festivities, left Elroy in the embrace of the Queen, subleased the two hostesses to the mayor and police chief who promised them keys to both the city and a condo on Hilton Head Island. Z.Z. and I made it back across the Florida border unscathed and unindicted.

A small victory perhaps, but a victory nonetheless.

nineteen

"Wherein our hero exacts a measure of revenge..."

Every now and then an opportunity comes along that makes that little devil that always dwells in the back of your mind claw and scratch his way into your consciousness. Such was the case the other day when Z.Z. and I took Natasha to the airport. She had an assignment to cover the Watermelon-Seed-Spitting Queen contest up in South Carolina; a state well-known for its pomp and pageantry.

Well, we drove her over to Edsel County International, dropped her at the terminal and decided to wait off the end of the runway for her plane to take off. We popped a couple of Manatee Malts and crawled up in the back of Z.Z.'s pickup truck. While we were waiting, this little old crop duster took off and went about ten feet over the top of us sounding like some kind of demented Everglades mosquito. Z.Z. snorted about half his Manatee up his nose and when he got through coughing and gagging said, "Jesus, Bubba! What the hell was that?"

That's when the mind went into overdrive and before I knew what I was saying, the mouth went into motion. "That, good buddy, was 'Buzz' Dolittle, war hero and aviator without peer! He could probably get a cypress stump off the ground and do a Cuban eight before it stalled!"

What I failed to mention at this point was that the war was with a rum bottle and his peers were either dead or institutionalized. Not to mention his record of being in more crashes than Evel Knievel.

Anyhow, Buzz is a cropduster pilot for one of those big farm conglomerates over in Homestead and spends most of his time breathing one or the other chemicals that are guaranteed to kill the various pests that threaten the local crops, not to mention what it does to the several thousand migrant workers that live along the path of the prevailing winds. They don't complain too much though as they consider a two-headed goat to be a sign of impending prosperity.

"Podner, that guy is hot! Man, I wish I'd gotten involved in something like that."

I knew right then that my buddy Z.Z. was ripe for the plucking.

"You don't know Buzz? I thought you knew every...body around here by now?" I'd almost said "every fool" but checked myself. "He's got a little two-seater that he takes out for fun and games. You want to go, I can fix it."

"Aw, Bubba. That'd be great!"

"Well, let me see what I can do tomorrow."

At this point, I would have promised Buzz Dolittle my first born or half my lottery winnings to take Z.Z. up for ten minutes. I had spent an eternity once (read about ninety seconds) in a plane which Buzz was flying, giving him the benefit of the doubt, and I had no intention of ever subjecting myself to that terror again. However, in Z.Z.'s case, I decided it was time for the payback from Hell.

Thus did it come about that a few days later, we found ourselves back at Edsel County International. Z.Z. had outfitted himself for this great flying adventure and damned if he didn't look a little like a fugitive from the Lafayette Escadrille, scarf and all. I had promised Buzz a six-pack of Mount Gay if they came back in one piece with the stipulation that one bottle was to be subtracted for every step Z.Z. could take away from the plane upon disembarking. I knew that Buzz would go for the full count.

To make it interesting, I insisted we have a couple of Bloody Marys on the way to the airport, just to celebrate this festive occasion, you understand.

Friends, have you ever heard of a hammerhead stall? That's when the plane goes straight up like the prop is winding around a piece of string until there ain't no more; then it starts to fall back on its tail until the nose falls over and it dives straight for the ground. Once that's done and the airspeed is screaming again, you pull up into a loop where you're upside down at the top then you're heading for the ground again. It's a thrill on a good day for an experienced flyer. For the novice with a gut full of Bloody Marys, it's unforgettable. Especially when it's done twice!

Buzz came out of the second loop over the end the runway at about fifty feet. I was a little worried about that one, but sure enough, he flared out, dropped her on the asphalt and that was that except for the ground loop he did right in front of the hangar to stop.

Well, quicker than you could say, "Houston, the Eagle has landed." Z.Z.hopped out and for a minute I was astonished at his vigor. Then I saw that he was wearing the tomato juice which made him look like he'd had a hatchet fight with Freddie Krueger. He took exactly one-half step and fell on his face. I told Buzz I wouldn't take a deduction from the rum for that feeble effort.

I drove Z.Z. home without either of us speaking and then I didn't see or hear from him for a couple of days. When I did finally run into him at "Sidepocket" Simpson's Pool Hall and Christian Reading Room, he was still a little green around the gills but he bought me a Manatee Malt and remarked, "That damn Buzz sure can fly that sucker, Bubba. I wonder where he got his training?"

I told Z.Z. how that brought back the memory of my flight with Buzz and how I'd sorta wondered the same thing out loud and Buzz had drawled, "What training?"

It was the better part of two weeks before Z.Z. spoke to me again. There's always calm before the storm.

twenty

"Wherein we begin a new year and new adventures..."

Happy New Year from all the folks down here in Edsel County! Another holiday season has come and gone and we managed to get through it with a minimum of scrapes and bruises. I guess about the worst thing that happened was the temporary breakup of Natasha and Z.Z.. At least, we hope it's temporary. They're speaking again but you could chill a six-pack with Natasha's attitude. It seems Z.Z. made some discreet inquiries on what to get Natasha for Christmas and it was pretty much unanimous that she expected a "big rock" from him. When he delivered a big old piece of coquina stone weighing about a hundred and fifty pounds and wrapped in a big red ribbon to her front porch, she broke a bottle of champagne over his head and wouldn't answer the phone for a week. Z.Z.'s only comment was, "How the hell was I supposed to know she meant a diamond?" Latest word is that he's made a standing offer to take her shopping at Baubles, Bangles and Bagels clearance store at the outlet mall. Maybe she'll give in.

We barely escaped losing the county's only doctor this year when Dr. K.K. (Knobby Knuckles) Nolan threatened to move his practice up to Palm Beach where he might get paid in real cash instead of eggs, produce and roadkill. Our county commissioners persuaded him to stay when they struck a bargain which guaranteed that Candy Jr. would show up every six months for a physical. The doctor in turn, promised to update his skills by taking some correspondence courses from the Larry Flynt School of Anatomy.

Speaking of Candy Jr., she's been putting the word out around town that she's available to provide solace to a certain local resident who's reputed to be raking in big bucks for songwriting royalties. I've been letting people know that I'm not sharing that fifty bucks a month with anybody. Though I might just let her talk me into introducing her to Billy Ray Muckenfuss, et al; it would be interesting to see who survived that match-up. I'd bet on an even match after the first two falls.

Katie's Conch House has been written up in all the slick magazines and is doing a land office business. Rumor had it that a bunch of New York actors were going to buy it and turn it into a disco/eatery called the "Upper West Side Soho Village Tavern on the Key". Katie told me that Bobby DeRigatoni and his lawyer Shelly "Shark" Shapiro had been in and were anxious to close the deal for the property. It seems J.C.(remember Juan Carlos, the maitre'd) overheard the conversation and made a counter offer on the spot which involved the northern intruders escaping with something called "cojones" and a warning that sounded like "Ju gyze beta pak ju azzes bak up nauth ip ju no wat be gud por ju, koz me an my prenz gone do dis deel!" (Read it slowly, it'll come to you.)

Anyhow, there's a sign in the parking lot that says, "Coming Soon! The Coca Cabana!" I guess they'll have girls walking around like the old days, "Cigars...cigarettes...13 round-9mm clip...?"

Katie said she and Sergeant Major are taking the money and moving to Key West where the people are normal. That's a stretch but, then again, everything's relative.

Speaking of real estate, remember I told you that Z.Z. and I had bought some swamp some years back? Well, somebody from up around Miami has been snooping around asking who owned it and stuff like that. I ran into Earlene Faye Edwards nee Stoudemeyer (my eighth grade flame) the other day and she told me that this guy had been looking through the tax rolls in the assessor's office where she works. He was taking a lot of notes and when he went to the bathroom, Earlene scoped out the page he was copying and, sure enough, it was our property. Z.Z. figures somebody wants to build a sport's arena on our site 'cause there's one on about every forty square miles of land around here.

"It's probably that guy up in Broward that owns all those teams already. I'll bet you he's got plans for another franchise; the National Bocce League or somethin'. Think about it...! The Edsel County Goombahs, World Bocce Champions! Won't be too many Rashaads or Neons on that team though...more like Dom, Vinnie and Patsy...good American names."

I told Z.Z. not to get his hopes up. More than likely the guy was from the EPA and we were gonna find out that we owned the world's biggest toxic waste dump.

In the meantime, Z.Z. says we need to make a few dollars and he's working on a surefire scheme to put some money in the bank while we wait for our real estate windfall.   I'm thinking of sneaking off to Costa Rica and changing my name. How's "El Bubba" sound?

twenty one

"Wherein gold and love clash..."

Lately I've been thinking about contradictions in history; like it was Thomas Jefferson who came up with "...all men are created equal..." yet old TJ owned a bunch of slaves and is *purported* (all lawyers please note the italicized disclaimer) to have fathered several children by one. This probably cost him a place on our folding money and resulted in his demotion to the nickel which is about one cut above being the trademark on a rubber heel.

What got me thinking about all this was an article from some slick magazine that Z.Z. dropped off the other day. Seems he's been reading up on this feller Mel Fisher who's been digging up the Florida Keys for years and finally found the wreck of the "Atocha", a Spanish treasure ship. Well, this article goes on to say that this little old ship was about a hundred-and-some feet long which is contradictory because anyone that's been in any gift shop anywhere near the keys knows that the Atocha had to be about the size of the Titanic to have carried all the stuff that's being sold as authentic

Spanish treasure from that ship. It doesn't even say, "Hecho en Peru" on most of it. So much for history.

Anyhow, Z.Z. says we've got to do a little research and find us a spot to go digging for dollars. I had to remind him that "digging" didn't exactly describe the process as all of those old wrecks were under considerable amounts of water not to mention a few centuries of coral buildup. "Hell, Bubba, I know that but I've already figured out a way to rig us up a sand blower and we've both got scuba gear so we're halfway there." Then he went on to describe how we'd rig a small generator and a Shop-Vac (set to blow not suck) in his boat and take turns on the business end of the hose.

They say that when you wake up from being hypnotized you don't remember what happened while you were under the trance. I figure that's the difference in the real thing and falling under Z.Z.'s spell. Unfortunately, every time one of his projects comes unglued, I remember it all too well. Such is the case with the great treasure hunt.

A couple of weeks after our conversation, dawn found us anchored on the reef off Marathon in the middle keys. Now dawn in the Florida keys is a beautiful thing to behold and gives every indication of nature and man at peace. That is until man decides to screw around with nature.

Experience had already proven that the combination of Z.Z., a boat and anything more complicated than a pocket comb was probably a deadly one. The day, however, was one of those chamber of commerce types when it was easy to be lulled into contentment and complacency.

Z.Z. allowed as how he'd make the first dive to check out the gear and scout the location. I fired up the generator and the Shop-Vac and fed the hose over the side of the boat to Z.Z. who immediately dropped from sight. Pretty soon, I could see a little cloud of sand floating away on the current so I figured the blower must be working fine. In a few minutes, Z.Z.'s head popped to the surface and as he spit out his mouthpiece he whooped, "Hot damn, Bubba! Just like I told you it would be. There's some timbers down there and a little shot with the hose clears the sand away real nice. I'm gone." And so he was.

Well, quicker than you could say, "Pinta! Nina! Santa Maria" he was back and this time he was clutching a chunk of coral in his hand and he was real quiet. "Bubba, look at this. Right here on the bottom. See that glint of metal through that crack?" Sure enough when I turned it over there was the dull shine of what could be gold reflecting the rising sun. "There must be a couple of dozen like this down there." "This" was about three inches square but wasn't particularly heavy which caused me to fantasize that these were probably a collection of gold medallions that had been packed in individual boxes. Z.Z. looked at me and winked and again dropped away.

Things were quiet for a few minutes and I figured that Z.Z. was probably just neatly stacking the gold prior to bringing it to the surface. I lost myself in pondering the value of a large gold medallion bearing the inscription "In Queen Isabella We Trust".

This reverie was broken by a rather insistent tugging on the vacuum hose and subsequent movement of the tank toward the side of the boat. Before I could react, the entire assembly was jerked over the side and immediately shorted out with great hissing and smoking. Meanwhile, the generator is still pumping 120 volts through the power cord into the seawater underneath the boat. By the time I managed to kill the power, Z.Z. had popped to the surface and was floating a few yards away in what appeared to be a semi-conscious state. I knew he was alive because he was moaning and sort of babbling. I jumped in and pulled him over to the boat and managed to strip him of his gear and get him aboard. I wasn't sure how much of a shock he'd received so I figured to get him to the doctor ASAP. Abandoning the gear and the gold, I lit out for Fisherman's Hospital in Marathon as fast as Z.Z.'s boat would run. It would be the next morning before I learned the true nature of his distress.

Seems that he was, in fact, stacking some more of his findings and had stuck the hose into his weight belt to secure it when a very large and ugly moray eel had decided that the vacuum hose was the life-mate he'd been seeking and, in a sudden fit of passion, had attached himself to the hose and Z.Z. His writhings panicked Z.Z. and also resulted in the dunking of the Shop-Vac and the subsequent shock which stunned them both. Fortunately, Z.Z.'s buoyancy vest had inflated and he had immediately surfaced. The eel's fate is not known but as Z.Z. would later remark, "I'll bet that the best that old eel's ever had!"

We decided to forego further treasure hunting when, after further examination of our recovered "gold medallions", they turned out to be the remains of a box of Mason jar lids that had probably fallen off a ship and washed up on the reef.

This whole experience has soured Z.Z. on "...that damned 'National Pornographic' magazine!" We'll see.

twenty two

"Wherein good triumphs over evil... temporarily..."

Somewhere down around Marathon, there's a big old moray eel that I would treat to a turkey if I could find him. Yeah, that same old moray that fell in love with Z.Z. and the vacuum hose. My buddy has been a little subdued since his encounter and/or near rape by that fella. Seems like one or the other of us winds up in the hospital after Z.Z.'s fund-raising efforts. Maybe we can enjoy some peace and quiet around Edsel County if he doesn't come up with any hare-brained schemes for a while.

The county hasn't been all that quiet in spite of Z.Z.'s tranquil manner; although one would expect tranquility when he's laid up.

The Coca Cabana opened to a great hoopla and pretty soon the traffic was heavy around the area. Within a few weeks, our local sheriff, "Sam" Kahunatuna, who was keeping a close eye on the operation, decided that all was not right, meaning that the stretch limos lined up across the parking lot kind of made him wonder if the conch chowder was really all that good. A discreet inspection of the contents of the Coca's dumpster revealed that very little food-like residue was making its way from the "restaurant". Champagne bottles and plastic baggies seemed to be the bulk of the detritus and Sam was quick to realize that not too many "early birds" patronized the place. There had been one older couple, however, that had wandered in there about five o'clock one afternoon seeking dinner. By the time Sam got there they were cavorting naked on the bayside beach.

I should take time to point out at this juncture that Sam (for Samoan) is about three-hundred pounds of retired Air Force military policeman and a three-tour Vietnam veteran who believes in the flag, mother and apple pie. Sam is about as American as anyone from Mobile, Moline or Montpelier. As Sam put it, "I'm bigger, browner, I've got more bullet holes in me than these little *maricones* and all I'm looking for is a little peace and quiet."

Edsel County has been the epitome of quiet since Sam took over and Z.Z.'s recent run-in over the gator is a case-in-point. Seems that Ol' Bogey is NOT a gator after all but is a Caiman which is closer to a crocodile but in any case is a highly protected critter. If Sam had let the wildlife people have Z.Z. they would have crucified him. Our sheriff, however, believes in keeping the "system' out of the loop whenever possible. Consequently, feeding Bogey for ninety days was Sam's way of exacting justice for our transgressions and insuring that we or, in this case Z.Z., understood just who was in charge.

Unfortunately for Juan Carlos and his friends, they just couldn't understand this concept until a failed attempt to booby-trap Sam's patrol car resulted in an inexplicable five-day power outage at the club. During the outage, someone jury-rigged some wiring to an outside generator and the resulting fire destroyed the building in a matter of minutes.

The chief of the Edsel County volunteer fire department, Pepe "Flaming" Figuroa denied claims that his firefighters had been watching a popular television star "coming out" on her weekly series thereby being slow to respond to the emergency. Sheriff Kahunatuna was supportive of the chief saying, "The chief and his troops were engaged in an intensive training session at the time of the fire. To my understanding, they were practicing an important rescue maneuver known as the 'fireman's drag' or 'fireman in drag' or some such."

So, the Coca Cabana is no more. Juan Carlos and his merry makers have disappeared and the latest word is that Katie and Sergeant Major are foreclosing on the land. We're all hoping for a new and improved Conch House before too long.

About the time that excitement died down, a rash of livestock killings started. Some of our Latin farmers had been losing goats and calves to what they call a "chupacabra" or "goat sucker". One or two farmers claimed to have seen the creature and described it as "...half man and half beast." When I jokingly told Natasha that the description sorta fit Z.Z., she said, "Yeah, and we know which half's which."

It's not unusual to find decapitated chickens, rabbits or goats around here because some of the locals practice a religion known as Santeria which holds on to the notion of animal sacrifice. At least they do it cleanly; this chupacabra sort of rips them up. I guess he goes to a different church.

Anyhow, Sheriff Sam is on the case and spends about half his time examining animal carcasses. He says he's pretty sure that when the hysteria dies down he'll find a couple of wild dogs running loose in the county. I figure he's right but I think I'll keep an eye on Z.Z. just the same.

twenty three

"Wherein failure is snatched from the jaws of success..."

Who ever said, "Idle hands are the devil's workshop." sure knew what he was talking about. Of course, I know WHO he was talking about. Z.Z., who else?

As I mentioned earlier, Z.Z. had been laid back since his encounter with the eel. He'd even been reading Shakespeare for relaxation. We were all hoping this was to be a kinder and gentler version of the old boy but his true colors would soon emerge.

A bunch of us went over to his place for possum chili one day after being warned by Natasha that he might act a little strange but we still weren't prepared for this new Z.Z. Every time he stirred the chili he'd holler, "Bubble, bubble, toil and trouble; fire burn and cauldron bubble..." Then, when he went to let the dog out, we got, "Out damned Spot, out I say..." Natasha took me aside and told me that he's been like this for a couple of weeks and it was driving her crazy. "Bubba, you've got to do something! You're his best friend." I allowed as how I would think about it and try to help her (and Z.Z.) out.

Later on, after we had eaten, the conversation got around to the latest chupacabra sighting and I noticed Z.Z. just sorta let the conversation go on around him; kind of like he was lost in thought. I watched him and wondered for a minute then thought to myself, "Aw, he can be a nut case sometimes but he doesn't have a mean or cruel bone in his body." Why, I'd seen him cry over a pelican that was tangled in some fishing line in a tree. When he couldn't get to him to set him free, he drove ten miles home, got his gun and put the big bird out of his misery. He couldn't stand the thought of the pelican suffering a slow death.

I didn't give it much thought for the next day or two, then I got a call. It took a couple of minutes for me to realize that I was hearing the old Z.Z. You know the one; "Now listen, Bubba. All we gotta do is...". I was so relieved at this turn of events that, in ten minutes time, I had agreed to another of his wild-assed adventures. This time, we were going to photograph the chupacabra!

It seems that hearing us talk about the beast the other day triggered his sense of adventure (I call it self-destruction) and he was off and running. He called the National Inquisitor (one of those supermarket scandal sheets) and asked what they'd pay for a picture of a chupacabra. Well, in short order, he had a guarantee of ten-thousand dollars for an un-retouched negative.

For a change, our logistical planning for an operation revealed no particular life-threatening equipment or circumstances. I briefly considered the nocturnal nature of the schedule, remembering the gator hunt, but my fears passed quickly. One would be hard-pressed to make a lethal combination from a couple of cameras, a bunch of flash bulbs and a female goat. Certainly, this would even challenge Z.Z.'s propensity for disaster.

The plan was simple; the last couple of attacks had occurred out by the county prison farm so this was the logical place to start. "Bubba, there's a scrub pine and palmetto thicket about half-a-mile past the farm that's perfect for us."

Z.Z. waxed enthusiastically. "We'll rig the cameras and flashbulbs in the afternoon then go back with the goat after dark." He had consulted the almanac to find a night with no moon and declared the coming Thursday to be ideal.

Thus, that afternoon found us at the selected spot which was perfect for our needs. The cameras were mounted on trees about fifteen feet apart and aimed at a point where we drove a length of 2" pipe in the ground for a tether. The flash bulbs were strung as high as our arms could reach with a fine connecting wire running from tree to tree then to a palmetto thicket some thirty or forty feet away. This would be our hiding place. That night, we would return with the goat, make the final preparations and once all was in readiness, extinguish the lights, lock the camera lenses open and using a red-lensed flashlight retire to the palmettos to begin our vigil.

As with any well-thought out plan, things went smoothly and by nightfall we were settled down in our bunker. Quietly, I might add which was difficult for us given our propensity for Manatee Malt and conversation.

Around ten o'clock, we heard the "lights out" siren from the farm and a few moments later, heavy breathing from the other side of the clearing. Z.Z. and I couldn't see each other though we were kneeling two feet apart so we had to rely on signals from the goat for the order to "fire". A couple of tentative bleats put us on "red alert" then a long plaintive cry followed by a hoarse "Uh! Uh! Uh!" galvanized us into action.

Z.Z. crossed the wires leading from the battery to the flashbulbs and our world exploded. Neither of us had thought to close or cover our eyes when the bulbs went off and the resulting fireworks show behind our eyelids was something to behold. It was a minute or two before we could even find the flashlight and, in the mean time, the chupacabra could be heard crashing through the brush heading for parts unknown.

As soon as we had closed the lens on the cameras, we lit the lantern literally shedding some light on the situation. The goat was excited but otherwise unharmed and we apparently had our picture. At last, we had completed a mission without hurting someone.

Now, do you honestly believe that all's well at this point and we're going to collect the ten grand? If you do, then you haven't been paying attention.

First thing next morning, we took the film to "Crotch"(don't ask) Cannon's photo lab for processing. Z.Z. said he trusted Cannon 'cause he knew where he kept his collection of photos of young girls. "If he messes with me," Z.Z. exclaimed "I'll put him away for eight-to-ten easy."

Soon, we could see in the wet negative the image of the goat with this figure hunched over it. Within minutes we had a large print in the soup and there was the final product. What a job we'd done; lighting, camera angle, exposure, all perfect. One minor detail was missing: the chupacabra.

What we had captured in minute detail was, as evidenced by his prison denims (the pants of which were down around his ankles), an escapee from the farm seeking relief from the first female he'd seen in ninety days.

We later learned through prison scuttlebutt that the escapee was one Gilles DeTrop, a French-Canadian doing time for exposing himself to an eighty-year-old lady up at Century Village. Further charges are pending as the lady laughed herself right into the hospital and the prognosis is said to be shaky.

Anyhow, word is that old Gilles about tore the gates down trying to get back into the farm. He has since become heavily involved in the farm's religious activities saying that

God gave him a sign by hurling lightning bolts at him. I guess we put a pretty good scare into that old boy. He is said to be giving serious consideration to the priesthood.

When Z.Z. heard this, he mumbled something about, "...goats and altar boys.", but I didn't get the connection.

twenty four

"Wherein a mystery ends and Cupid strikes..."

Well, it turns out Sheriff Sam was right about the chupacabra. A couple of days after our attempt at photographing the beast, Sam got a call from old Mrs. Smyth out on the by-pass. It was about ten o'clock at night and something was riling up the chickens and livestock. Sam hustled out there and had no sooner pulled up in the yard than a couple of young goats came tearing around the corner of the house and jumped up on the roof of Sam's brand-new Cadillac patrol car (Rumor has it that Katie bought it for him as a reward for running Juan Carlos out of town.) where they commenced to do a tap dance on that nice metallic pearl finish.

Just as Sam started to get out of the car, here comes two of the biggest, meanest looking pit bulls that anybody's ever seen. The dogs ran up to the car and stood up on their hind legs to snap at the goats, meanwhile clawing hell out of the side of the car. Now Sam is on the horns of a dilemma. He certainly can't open the door or window but if he doesn't do something soon the goats and dogs are going to rip his car apart.

The sheriff, known for decisive action in times of crisis, simply whipped out his 9mm Glock and shot both dogs...through the front and back windows on the driver's side.

Now Sam is back driving the army-surplus jeep that the county provides him while the Caddie is up in Miami getting new windows and a paint job. The up side of this is that there have been no more chupacabra sightings. Case Closed.

Oh, before I forget, Natasha and Z.Z. got formally engaged. Yep, with a diamond and everything. We threw a big party for them at Katie's to celebrate that and the grand opening of the new restaurant. Katie's is back in business again. Again is not exactly right though cause the whole thing is brand new; even the name. How does "The Casa Caterina Cafe and Fern Bar" grab you?

Z.Z. doesn't think much of the concept and says that, "...sitting in Caterina's is about like drinking in a mangrove thicket give or take a few mosquitoes and raccoons." I've had to remind him once or twice that although he's always bitchin' about "...those yuppy tourist scum.", he's been spotted in there more than once in loafers, chinos and a shirt with an alligator on it.

"Bubba, that's no 'gator. That's a Caiman and I wear it in honor of our worthy opponent, Ol' Bogey. Even Sheriff Sam said it was a nice gesture."

I also have to remind him from time to time that he's spoken for and shouldn't be in there chasing the schoolteachers and secretaries that come down from Dade for a little weekend action. He rationalizes this by figuring that Natasha is the one wearing a ring, not him. If Natasha catches him, more than his logic is going to be twisted.

I suppose this might be a good place for a little update on my love life or lack of same.

At the engagement party, Natasha asked me if I'd been around the county library lately and when I told her that I really hadn't had much time to read "War and Peace" recently, she said that I might want to check it out.

Knowing Natasha as I do, I read between the lines and figured she had more in mind than my literary education. So I scheduled a trip to the Edsel County Library and Baseball Card Emporium. The librarian, Miss Fern Maynard, had been there as long as anyone alive could remember and Miss Fern was still holding down the fort. Though everyone called her "Miss Fern", she never used first names and until well into my majority I had been addressed as "Young Mister Convoy". She lost the "young" part about time I quit parting what was left of my hair. The only time I ever heard her utter the word "Patrick" was when she called my mother once to express her concern over, "...the inordinate interest in Gray's Anatomy being shown by Patrick and Clyde." Z.Z. and I had been unable to gain access to Playboy at the time.

Anyhow, Miss Fern expressed her pleasure at seeing me as this was her last week on the job. She was retiring to travel and see the world meaning most everything north of the Tamiami Trail.

"Mister Convoy, I want you to meet the new librarian, Miss Fenwick; Melanie Fenwick. Let me find her; she's back in the stacks somewhere."

Now librarians don't come with names like Melanie; it's more like Millicent or Olga or something. Girls named Melanie don't wear granny glasses and hair buns with pencils sticking out of them. Neither did this one! Melanie doesn't quite describe her. What I saw was Debussy! What I heard was Tchaikovsky! What I was thinking of was Ravel! In other words, what I saw was an auburn-haired apparition with sea-green eyes. What I heard was the 1812 Overture with my heart doing the cannons. What I was thinking of was doing the Bolero with her. This was no simple Melanie; this was a symphony.

The introductions concluded, it was determined that Miss Fenwick had tired of working in a large metropolitan library where she spent the day dodging drunks and derelicts so she opted for a simpler life in Edsel County. Her new life might be a lot simpler but I knew that mine was going to be a damned sight more complicated from this moment on.

Needless to say, after three weeks, I was up to number six on the Times bestseller list and had practically memorized the Dewey Decimal System. Z.Z. says the only reason that I haven't taken up pipe-smoking is that she wouldn't let me do it in the library. I like to think of my life as a series of small successes. While I still call her Miss Fenwick; she already calls me Patrick.

twenty five

"Wherein our hero carries a torch..."

We're not talking the Olympics here. Ol' Bubba has done gone and fell for the new county librarian. I mean like ass over teakettle. He's one sorry sight to see these days what with moping around town with his nose stuck in a book and his eyes looking like something out of a triple-A road atlas. Before long, he'll be needing glasses and not because of what his mama warned him about.

On the other hand, I can't say that I blame him 'cause that Melanie is sure enough something to look at. If I didn't already have Natasha going for me, I must might take up some heavy reading myself. Speaking of Natasha, she said she overheard Candy Jr. the other day telling somebody that Melanie, "...wasn't any great shakes." Natasha wondered if Candy Jr. went by the library to check her out. "If she did, that's the closest she's been to a book since eighth grade when she got hold of a copy of Erica Jong's 'Fear of Flying'. She heard it was one of those 'How to...' books."

I allowed as how Candy Jr. ought to be glad that when they made Melanie they didn't break the mold 'cause she was next off that assembly line. Natasha agrees that about the only difference is that Melanie's hair and eyes are their natural color and she's got a brain. I knew it was time for me to shut up when I almost said that none of that made much difference in the dark.

It's taken me a while to get Natasha to the point where she's stopped calling me "Clyde" with an icicle hanging on the end of it. I do love that gal even if she does get a little touchy now and then. The other day, I got a little held up over at Katie's, I mean Caterina's, and I called to tell her I'd be a little late for supper and to just keep it warm in the oven. Now, a reasonable woman would have told me it was a salad.

I don't think it's PMS though; more like WTW as in 'When's the wedding?". I've tried to explain to her that there's not going to be one as long as she insists that I'm gonna have to wear socks that day. Sometimes a man just has to stand up for what's right.

Anyhow, I think it's about time that me and Bubba made a little therapeutic field trip. He's been so out of it lately that he almost had a head-on collision in the car wash the other day.

There's a big golf tournament coming up at Rugrat Plantation on Hilton Head Island and one of our old high-school buddies, Tommy Lee "Shank" Bunker is the assistant pro at Sand Spur Dunes Country Club and Rehab Clinic where the tournament is being played. Shank says he can put us up for a few days and get us clubhouse passes so we can hobnob with the Tigers and Sharks and maybe even the Bear. I meant to ask Shank what kind of animal a Vijay was but I forgot.

If I can get Bubba up there maybe it'll take his mind off Melanie just a little bit. Do him good to get out in the sun every day and maybe work up his appetite. Besides, I got a little surprise lined up for his libido.

A couple of weeks ago, I got a postcard from Astrud and Gunilla. You remember, they're the two bim..er, models that we took up to South Carolina a little while back. Well, it seems they're still in the condo up there at Hilton Head while the ex-mayor and the ex-police chief do a little white-collar time at the Club Fed in Tampa. Something about a million-dollar kickback on a new city hall/jail. It's one thing to take graft; another not to pay taxes on it.

So, I called the girls and they're having open house during the tournament and we're invited. I reckon if anybody asks, we'd better tell them we'll be at Shank's.

The only possible glitch I can see right now is Bubba's date this coming Friday night. He finally got up enough nerve to ask Melanie to go out to dinner with him and if all goes well, I may not be able to pry him away from her. We'll have to wait and see. I'll bet you one thing though; Madame Librarian ain't lettin' Bubba's fingers do the walking through her pages anytime soon. That one's a hard cover in a paperback world.

Anyhow, I'm trying to turn Bubba's damper down a little bit.

"Fore" and all that golf jazz.

twenty six

"Wherein ambitions are realized...in spades..."

It was the best of times...it was the worst of times. Whoa! Got a little carried away there. That Chuck Dickens is a trip, isn't he? I'm through the D's and E's now and figure to start on the F's any day now. Miss Fenwick, the librarian, says that fellow Fitzgerald is a little dated but is still a tall dog in, as she says, "...American belles-lettres." I sure hope he wrote some hot love letters 'cause I'm getting a little bored with this literature business.

You see, since our last visit, I've been spending my spare time, actually most of my time, at the county library. In addition to cramming my brain with books, I've developed a new motor skill. I can pretty much read with one eye and keep the other on Miss Fenwick. Just between you and me, I couldn't give a rat's ass about the books; it's her I've been trying to read.

The minute I laid eyes on her I knew that my education was lacking and I wanted to do a little homework with that thing. Since she came here two months ago it's been difficult to think about much else. Z.Z. says he's getting tired of watching me watching her.

"Bubba, if you had any sense, you'd take her to Katie's, I mean Caterina's, feed her a couple or three of those Rum-Runners and talk her out of her knickers before she pukes or passes out."

I tried to explain to him that I didn't view her through carnal eyes and that my intentions were honorable. His comment was, "Bull, the first time you get closer than two feet from her, you'll be pawing the ground and snortin' like some horny moose." That didn't happen but it was a trial.

I finally got up enough nerve to ask Miss Fenwick for a date and she agreed on the condition that I start calling her Melanie instead of Miss Fenwick. When I said she could call me Bubba she allowed as how she'd stick with Patrick for the time being. I could live with that.

Well, we went to Katie's, I mean Caterina's, and Melanie started out by ordering a dozen oysters on the halfshell which she insisted we split. This was followed by a big old Caesar Salad and an ostrich steak and a half of a Katie's Key Kumquat Pie. All this was washed down with a couple of martinis and a bottle of Okeefenokee Brackish Sauvignon. Then she wanted to dance; hell, I couldn't walk!

She managed to stand me up and waltz me around for a few minutes then said, "Patrick, you look like you could use a cup of coffee. Let's go to my place." I was too far gone to appreciate what was happening and, in fact, everything is pretty hazy from that point on. I do seem to remember something about being on her couch and her over me with her eyes all scrunched up and hollerin', "Gaaawd! BUUUUUUBBBAAAAAaaaaaaaaa...!!!"

Somehow, I found my way home about daylight and when I woke up about four o'clock, there was a message on my machine: "...and don't forget to ask Katie for a refund on those oysters. You ate six and only four worked." I'll take her word for it.

Whoever said, "Be careful what you wish for; you just might get it." sure as hell knew what he was talking about and these last few days, I've learned about "...too much of a good thing."

Anyhow, it seems advisable to take a bit of a break about now and get a little fresh air in the lungs. I've been digging in that book mine too long. Z.Z. says he's been in touch with our old buddy Shank Bunker up at Hilton Head and that Shank wants us to come up for the big professional golf tournament at Sand Spur Dunes where he's the assistant pro. Sounds like that might just be the rest and relaxation that I sorely need so I guess I'll sign on for the trip. Like ol' Bing Crosby used to sing "...straight down the middle...".!

twenty seven

"Wherein travels are resumed and trouble may be assumed..."

Neither one of us had ever been big golf fans and Z.Z. had always liked shooting pool better 'cause, as he says, "In a good pool hall, you're never more than twenty feet away from a beer in one direction and the men's room in the other."

Our only flurry of real interest had come several years ago when ol' Shank almost played himself into the U.S. Open. He was leading by four strokes with three holes to go in a final qualifying round when one of a pair of drop-dead twin debutramps in the gallery passed him a note. It seems the note described in explicit clinical detail just what the twins wanted to do with Shank as soon as he finished his round. Well, Shank played the last three holes six over par and lost by two strokes to Vic "The Weasel" Womack who, as it turned out, was the twins' older brother. Weasel went on to win two majors and finish in the top ten on the money list for two years running.

Weasel's success came to a sudden end when the twins were banned from every pro tournament in the country and Rocco Fagioli's backers threatened to qualify Weasel for the ladies' tour. (Sports footnote: Rocco finished second in both of Weasel's major wins.) Last anyone heard, Weasel was running a driving range on Okinawa.

Shank tried the Nike tour for a year or so but gave it up when the Sand Spur Dunes offer came along. He says now he's living in a condo instead of his car, eating and drinking high on the hog and specializing in teaching young lovelies from Charlotte and Atlanta how to improve their grips.

Unfortunately, we couldn't get away in time to get up to Hilton Head and catch a Wednesday practice round. Shank says that's when you get the best golf 'cause the pros are making bets and ragging on each other; that is, when they're not looking to see whose gonna be their Miss Nineteenth Hole. They like to get the choices out of the way before the shooting starts on Thursday. This was the result of the Womack sisters affair. If a golfer could get himself a decent motel caddie who could read the label on a bottle of Bombay and the nasty left-to-right break on a king-size bed, then he wouldn't be tempted by some sand-trap siren when he was in the middle of business; like trying to draw a five iron over the marsh and onto the upper terrace of the eighteenth green for a chance at a match-winning birdie.

It was an all-day haul up to Hilton Head but for once, I-95 was reasonably calm. There was some kind of roadblock up around Daytona Beach but I didn't see anybody pulled over that didn't look like an importer of fine Colombian pharmaceuticals, i.e., relatively young, black or Hispanic, and driving anything newer than an AMC Gremlin.

We got to Rugrat Plantation about five in the afternoon and when we called Shank, he said he'd be in the bar at the marina by the time we got there. Well, we followed the signs to what was called Captain Charlie's Marina and after looking for a parking place for a half hour, finally just parked in some trees and headed toward the water. Getting to the marina was like trying to wade through the playground of a daycare center. There were house apes everywhere. We managed to dodge the ice cream cones and strollers and found the bar under a small lighthouse. Shank was waiting for us and after a little back-slapping and high-fivin', we settled down for some quality bar-time.

After a lovely dinner of stale pretzels and popcorn, the talent started arriving and serious food was out of the question when the buffet of Tammi, Sheri, Jodi, etc., showed up. Shank had to restrain Z.Z., or I should say, had to explain to Z.Z. that these were local girls and one didn't mess with them unless one was dead serious; as in matrimony. The unwritten rule was the locals kept each other out of trouble and while they would drink and party together, they were off-limits.

"Besides, by tomorrow night, there'll be more little out-of-town stroke-savers in here than you can shake a titanium shaft at." Shank was pretty deft in the vernacular.

The next morning, after a breakfast of coffee and Bromo-Seltzer, we wandered over to the golf course to see what was happening. Shank was busier than a one-legged kick boxer trying to keep the pros, press and club members out of each others way. He gave us our passes and told us we were on our own until sunset.

"Be sure you're at the marina bar then," he said, "That's when we'll find us some serious low-handicap playing partners for the evening."

We managed to rustle us up a couple of milkshake cups full of Bloody Mary and then we headed for the course.

Now walking around a golf course with a serious case of the Bombay flu ranks right up there with a visit to the proctologist on my list of favorite things to do. We did manage to pay our respects to Tom, Curtis, Nick and Payne and even got to swap hellos with Fuzzy. He might as well have been out walking the dog 'cause he just sauntered along whistling and exchanging pleasantries with the few spectators he encountered. Shank said later there was about twelve thousand people on the course that day but eleven-thousand-nine-hundred-ninety of them were following Tiger. We decided to break for lunch and maybe a little nap before our sunset tee time.

Later on when we were getting dressed, I knew this was going to be an interesting evening. Z.Z. had come up with a pair of argyle knickers, a chartreuse ban-lon shirt and white kiltie loafers. The finishing touch to this ensemble was one of Shank's old golf gloves hanging out of his hip pocket as if casually forgotten after the day's round. I told him that it wasn't going to take a Rhodes scholar to see through this get-up. His reply was, "Bubba, they ain't likely to be any where we're going and besides, I'll damn sure look different from all those guys wearing horses." I couldn't argue that point. Time would prove the wisdom of his thinking.

twenty eight

"Wherein debts are paid and it's deja vu all over again..."

Fans, I've seen the pit bunnies at the big sports car races; the hotel lobby hangers-on during Super Bowl week and I even went to a cheerleader tryout for the Edsel County Armadillos last year but for sheer quality I believe it's hard to beat the pro golf tour. After Thursday's round, we hadn't been in the bar for more than half a drink when the place filled up with what ol' Dan Jenkins called, "steel-bellied home wreckers". The closest thing to this collection of first-class bimbettes that I'd ever seen was when I stumbled into a plastic surgeon's convention in Boca Raton one time. The big difference here was the amount of what appeared to be "natural talent", not that anybody was going to call his broker the next morning and dump his silicone stock.

Soon we were joined by Shank and Percy Smyth-Churchill, an Englishman new on the American tour. He and Shank had been buddies for a couple of years since trying to qualify for the tour. Young Percy looked just like the guy you went to high school with that was president of the debating club or ran the movie projector. Shank was quick to point out, however, that Percy had been a pure stud on the course that day and had managed to hit every fairway and drain a few putts for a fine 68 which had him up on the leader board tied for fourth. The buzz went around the room quickly and soon we had quite a gallery. Z.Z. made sure to stick close to Percy in order to be close to the center of the action. I heard him remark to one of the cuties something about, "...just came off the practice tee and didn't have time to change." Shank and I just sorta sat back and handicapped the fillies.

It didn't take long for Percy and Z.Z. to end the qualifying and announce their departure for dinner and a good night's rest in preparation for the next day's round. The two lovelies they left with looked like they knew how to keep their heads down and follow through. When I expressed some concern about Percy's welfare, Shank assured me that Percy was serious about his game and could be trusted to be ready to go tomorrow. What I failed to enter into the equation at that moment was Z.Z. I never learn.

Shank and I decided to call it an early evening as he had been on the go since daylight and I was still recovering from an overdose of Melanie.

Z.Z.'s absence on Friday morning was of no particular concern, in fact, I would have been surprised had he been there. The fact that Percy wasn't on the practice tee by 8:30 was cause for alarm, however, and Shank put out an APB about 9 o'clock. With a 10:05 starting time, it was becoming clear that even if Percy turned up, he was going to have to start cold.

We had just about given up when one of the caddies shouted that Percy had been spotted dashing from pine tree to pine tree out behind the clubhouse. Thus it was, with fifteen minutes to go, a nearly naked Percy was rushed into the locker room, dressed out in borrowed pants and shirt and half-carried to the first tee. After a couple of practice swings, Percy was up and somehow managed to hit a duck hook into the gallery about seventy-five yards down the fairway. That was one of his better shots on the front nine. After eight consecutive bogies, he somehow managed to find himself on number nine and tap-in for a par. That and a cold beer that he inhaled on the way to the next tee seemed to do the trick and he was able to finish the back nine in par to go four-over and make the cut. Later, Percy would swear that he had no recollection of the front nine holes.

Thankfully, the wind came up on Saturday and the Americans, trying to play their flop and stop game, were all over the place. Percy, on the other hand, was accustomed to playing Europe's goat pastures and managed to punch his way to a 69 and a one-over through fifty-four holes which put him five back of the leader who just happened to be Rocco Fagioli. Fate is a cruel mistress.

I forgot to mention that it was about noon on Friday when Z.Z. surfaced again. Seems that on Thursday night, he and Percy wound up on a yacht with the two girls where they partied until the wee smalls. Awakened by the sound of the engines, Percy had jumped ashore leaving his clothes and Z.Z. somewhere in the bowels of the ship. When Z.Z. inally came to, land was a shadow on the horizon and he was on his way to Charleston. Luckily, it didn't take him long to hitchhike back. Dressed as he was, there wasn't much doubt where he was headed.

On Sunday, with a decent round and a good night's rest behind him, Percy was all business on the practice tee. Shank says that when Percy's game is on, he can hit his irons into a teacup. Just before he teed off, Percy said he felt like he could throw a pretty good score up on the board and make the eight golfers behind him work a little.

Well, all little ol' Percy did was go out there and shoot your basic 64, which if his tee shot hadn't hit the pin on the par-3 sixteenth and bounced out would have been a course record

63. Seven-under in the clubhouse was a decent place to be on this Sunday afternoon as six of the remaining golfers had shot themselves in the foot with the bogies flying thick and fast. Only the last twosome, Rocco Fagioli and Kosha Tofu from Japan were playing decent golf. They'd started the round tied at four under and finished the front nine with a couple of birdies each. Two golfers at six-under with nine to go could be a problem.

Through the next five holes, neither golfer could get the juices flowing, then on number sixteen, Tofu hit a shot identical to Percy's only it hit the pin and dropped in for a hole in one. Rocco, not to be outdone, flopped one behind the hole that bit, rolled back over the hole and stopped eight inches below for a tap-in.

By now, in the clubhouse, Percy's throwing up, Shank's fingernails are gone and I'm thinking that a little Bombay anasthesia is in order.   Then on the par-5 seventeenth, lightning strikes. Tofu pulls his drive into the trees and has to punch out to the fairway making for a real tough par. Rocco is long down the middle and starting to feel the adrenaline rush. A birdie and a par and it's his tournament.   Sure enough, Tofu's next shot is to the bunker at the back of the green and from there he couldn't pick it up and walk it down in two. Rocco lays up, hits his pitch a little fat and has a ten-footer for the birdie. Tofu finally get down in six bringing him back to seven under. Rocco strokes a putt that needed about one-eighth inch more break, rolls around the lip and comes back at him. Tap-in for par.

Shank says that a birdie on eighteen requires divine intervention and we might as well plan on a sudden death playoff.   Percy and Shank headed for the practice tee; I ordered a double.

About this time, Z.Z. showed up from touring the local flora and fauna and it's obvious he doesn't have the big picture.

"Yo, Bubba.   You ready to drink some of Percy's champagne?"

When I pointed out that a two or three-way playoff was likely, he was downright philosophical.

"Well, I reckon that ol' number eighteen can be a four-hundred-and-eighty-yard minefield."

It was a made for television finish.

Both players hit their drives down the middle so close together you could have covered them with a handkerchief. Both hit second shots to the front of the green some thirty-five feet from the pin.   Get down in two and let's go for a walk back to sixteen.

Z.Z.'s got his feet up on the table and I hear this kind of sigh from him,"Yessssss..."

Tofu's away so he squats; he squints; he straightens up and wipes his glasses then squats again.   Finally he addresses the putt...and skulls it!   The ball goes about six feet.   Rocco's turn: he squats; he squints; straightens up and immediately whacks the ball fifteen feet past the hole nearly to the back fringe. Tofu's turn again: without even looking at the line, he strikes a nice putt that slides by on the high side. Tap-in for a bogey five and second place. Rocco again: having never moved from where he hit the first putt, he takes a deep breath and trudges up the green to his ball; another deep breath and he strokes on a perfect line, dead center.   One more turn of the ball...but...IT STOPS! Half in, half out. Waiting for it to turn but it's dead. Bogey!

Silence for a full minute.   The television goes to split screen; one camera on the ball; the other on Rocco. Suddenly there's movement behind him.   Familiar faces standing up from where they'd been crouched on the green's fringe. It's Astrud and Gunilla in identical spandex mini-dresses; smiling; hugging each other.

Z.Z. stood, exhaling another "Yessss..." then adding "Here, Bubba, give these to Percy for his trophy case. I figured I owed him for the other night."

It took me a moment to realize I was holding two pairs of bikini panties.

twenty nine

"Wherein riches are realized and reneged..."

Sometime Monday afternoon, I woke up from the Sunday Night Massacre which is what we came to call the party after Percy's win. By then, all the Gingers, Erins and Pams had departed from Shank's condo taking most of their clothes with them. Percy had departed for rehab where he was going to dry out and start building up his strength for the Masters in Augusta.

For those of you who might not know, the Masters is where golfers who are not into whips and chains go for a session of self-flagellation. You know, where you shoot three consecutive 67's then a big old 90 grabs you by the short and curlies on Sunday afternoon.

We later learned that Astrud and Gunilla had beat a hasty departure with an Australian golfer nicknamed "The 'Roo" 'cause he always jumped up and down every time he made a halfway decent shot. Seems he'd been rather successful at second place choke finishes and a line of clothing with his nickname on the label. I didn't care much for his styling though as everything including the hats had pouches on them. Anyhow, he had this big old yacht and was headed south so the girls signed on for the trip home to South Beach.

Shank had to clean up some loose ends from the tournament but said he thought he'd try to get down to Edsel County soon as he needed a break from the pastel pants and duck hook crowd.

"Besides," he said, "I'm tired of those damn Junior Leaguers pushing strollers around with their one-point-seven-five rugrats and waving their wedding rings like they was some kind of award for bravery. Hell, we know what the reward was for and once they got that ring there's no more gobbling ol' Junior. After the second kid, most of them become born-again virgins anyhow."

It's hard to argue with a truly dedicated philosopher.

Z.Z. and I decided to wait until Wednesday to head for Edsel County figuring the scratches and bruises wouldn't look so bad after another day. Besides, we knew we'd better be well rested when we got home 'cause Natasha Sue and Melanie would undoubtedly put us to the test. You know, the one where you have to grab'em when you walk through the door and start panting and snorting like you haven't seen a woman in about six months. If you're lucky, you can take care of business with minimum removal of your clothes thereby giving any incriminating bite marks another day to heal.

I guess the big news is the registered letters that Z.Z. and I had waiting for us when we got home. Seems I was right about some folks wanting to buy our mangrove swamp...uh...valuable property that I mentioned a while back and the letter contained an initial offer in the high six-figure bracket. We have engaged the services of one T.J. "Toe Jam" Jones, Esq. to negotiate with the prospective buyers. Now Toe Jam doesn't look like much with his one blue seersucker suit and all (he gets it cleaned once a week whether it needs it or not) but he can flat-out get in some of those big-time lawyers knickers when he sets his mind to it.

When that big home improvement outfit, Commode Boutique, wanted to build out on the by-pass, Toe Jam negotiated their butts into paying ten times what they'd initially offered the Widow Tucker for her ten acres. Some people got a little upset when they learned he kept a little over half the money but all was forgiven when he married the widow's cross-eyed step-daughter. Only the most cynical folks around figured he was trying to get it all. Anyhow, he told us to wait and countered with an offer that made Z.Z. hyperventilate and gave me a giggling fit. We told him if he got anywhere near that much, he was damn-well welcome to half of it. We'll see, we'll see.

In anticipation of our possible new-found riches, Z.Z. suggested we motor up to Miami Beach to the annual International Boat Show. After the bout with Ol' Bogey and the eel encounter, Z.Z's old boat was a little the worse for wear so it seemed reasonable to invest some funds in something a little more befitting our status, not to mention one that might survive a casual day on the water.

Now folks in the know realize that the hype surrounding a boat show only scratches the surface and there's a lot more to the fun and games than meets the eye. That's why it's otherwise known as the annual Rolex and silicone-rack showdown. There's lots of fun events ranging from "watch that six-foot blonde in the mini-skirt climb that ladder and watch that same blonde when she hits the air conditioning" to multiple choice games like "Is that (a)his niece, (b)daughter, (c)third wife or (d)just a hired gun for the weekend?" A Rolex is not the only well-oiled machine that Bernie Bigbucks has on his arm.

Z.Z.'s idea was that we'd check out the main show, shop the hardware in our price bracket, meaning something that could be pulled behind a pickup truck, then mosey on over to Collins Avenue where the seven and eight-figure skiffs were on sale.

"Bubba, we'll see some fine examples of American plastic surgery and maybe even a few natural wonders while we're at it. Hell, if we clean up some, we might even manage to tie up alongside a couple of 'em for the evening." Z.Z.'s nothing if not the eternal optimist.

Thus, the following week found us amongst the filthy rich, the nouveau rich, the not-so-rich and the downright poor. Toe Jam hadn't received a reply to his counter offer yet so we weren't sure how much money we could spend but we agreed that we'd just find a boat that met our needs and not one that would bankrupt us. Of course, my needs and those of the esteemed Mr. Ryder were polar opposites. I thought that a twenty-five to thirty footer with twin-outboards, a small cuddy cabin with miniature head and cushions and someplace to store rods and diving gear would fill the bill. Z.Z. was leaning more toward something of forty plus feet capable of speeds in excess of seventy-five miles an hour while carrying a full keg of beer and three or four severely underdressed women. He allowed as how, under those circumstances, he'd just as soon forget about fishing and diving, at least under water.

Well, we picked up about a hundred pounds of brochures from the dealers with the idea of going over them at our leisure and making an intelligent decision about our purchase. Translated: we'd get half in the bag, argue for an hour and wind up flipping a coin to see who got to pick.

One thing I forgot to mention; remember Z.Z.'S get-up at Hilton Head? This time, he outdid himself as only someone trying to look "yachtie" can. Where he finds this stuff, I'll never know but if there's a "Tacky Togs" outlet somewhere, he'll damn sure find it. How's this strike you?

A captain's hat of the ninety-nine-cent Woolworth variety, a white shirt with a collar that looked like the hat worn by the "Flying Nun"; around his neck was what was purported to be an ascot but was, in reality, a bandanna; white, bell-bottomed polyester trousers and what looked like a pair of majorette boots with tassels. When questioned about the practicality of boat shoes, he informed me that serious boaters take off their shoes before boarding anyway so what difference did it make. I could only wonder what passersby would think taking place on a boat where those boots rested by the gangway.

Actually, we found out pretty quick that Z.Z. fit right in with most of the gawkers at the show and even the big-time brokers figured him for some kinda eccentric billionaire from God-knows-where. Fortunately, by the time we got over to the big in-the-water show in front of the Fontainebleu Hotel (the Fart-and-Blow as Z.Z. called it), he had deep-sixed the boots in favor of a pair of lizard-skin boat shoes, lost the cheap cap and swapped the god-awful collar for a tee-shirt he'd picked up at one of the booths. It pictured a young lovely with her thong-encased derriere thrust out, beneath which was the logo of K-Y Tropic Suntan Lotion. In spite of what you think, it was an improvement.

Let me say right here that the big boys know how to do it up right! We saw boats, I use the term 'boats' advisedly, that while they didn't have a lot more square footage than your average double-wide, had a few more of what you call your amenities. Maybe I should use the term yacht as opposed to boat. I guess a boat is something you can jump off of to take a whiz and get a bath at the same time. Your basic little yacht has got a Jacuzzi for everybody, including the dog, and also has those funny little water fountains for sitting on. I guess it's a girl thing.

Anyhow, before you could say, "Thank you, Dow-Jones!", we were ensconced in the lap of wretched excess and the broker, Biff Taffrail, was waving a contract under our noses for what was either a yacht or the state of Rhode Island, the square footage being equal and all. We figured we'd better check in with Toe Jam for the latest status on our bottom line.

You know what's coming, right?

It seems that while our esteemed counsel had been negotiating for some exorbitant price for the swam...property, the Feds had been making an end run and it was now designated federal wetlands. The EPA, Interior Department, Corps of Engineers and about every other agency short of the Secret Service had gotten together and decided that this was too valuable a natural asset to be paved over. Hell, from now on, an osprey would need a permit to build a nest. Consequently, it had been decided to return to us the fair value of the parcel, meaning what we paid for it. Therefore, a check was in the mail for sixteen-hundred dollars; payable, of course to our escrow account, meaning Toe Jam was going to get his hands on the money first.

Luckily, Toe Jam was reasonable about the whole thing and said that he wouldn't take but a third for his fee seeing as how he had advised us to hold out for top dollar. He felt real bad about us not walking away with a couple of hundred thou apiece, himself included.

Thus it was that our champagne and caviar dreams were put to rest, not to mention that we were unceremoniously dumped on the dock by Biff the broker

Z.Z. waxed philosophical as we were tossed:

"Hell, Bubba, I'm not sure my ol' pickup woulda pulled that thing on a trailer anyhow!"

Sometimes, you gotta love him...

thirty

"Wherein the stage is set for further troubles..."

Boy, our days as real estate tycoons were sure short-lived but the government paid up in short order and to our surprise old Toe Jam had done a job on them and somehow jacked the rascals up into six-figures which meant we were all in tall cotton.   After our esteemed attorney's cut, there was still enough left over for us to pick up a decent fishing boat and have enough left over to show the girls a good time.

Natasha was lobbying hard for a down payment on the proverbial vine-covered cottage for the day when she and Z.Z. finally did the deed. Meanwhile, Z.Z. was leaning more toward a bayside condo known mostly for a plethora of time-sharing female yuppies outta Broward County.

Other than my share of the boat purchase, I had no plans for the remaining funds though it was a good bet that I would probably need to go to Switzerland and get those monkey gland shots or the sheep what-evers to keep up with Melanie. I was beginning to get the idea that her philosophy was if you just ordered-in Chinese, pizza or whatever, you didn't need clothes or a car. It had never occurred to me that sex was economical. Seems it was always the other way around what with having to wine and dine the latest object of your desire.

Lust equals expensive was the way I'd always viewed the equation. I knew the wisdom behind the old saying, "Every time a pretty girl smiles, a man's wallet weeps.". Lord knows, I'd seen my wallet break out in wracking sobs more than once. Now it seems I was willing to pay whatever price to escape exactly that which was nearly free.

Fortunately, Melanie still had her job at the library which meant I could sneak down to Katie's for a Manatee Malt and some lunch most days. Yeah, it was Katie's again much to the relief of all the locals who had gotten damned tired of all the tourons taking up space and yakking on their cellular phones to the folks back in the frozen north. Katie had finally banned the damned things and threatened to fire any employee that allowed the TV set to be turned to any channel that showed the Dow-Jones average.

The big sign out front had been replaced when one of our esteemed county commissioners, Sanford Mims, had taken it out with his El Dorado while trying to negotiate a turn onto the highway. Seems that the Honorable Mr. Mims was attempting to avoid a confrontation with Mrs. Mims over the presence in his car of one lightly-clad Bambi LaBoom who, at the time, was purportedly searching for an object or objects under the driver's-side seat.

Anyway, the sign came down, the commish escaped his wife's immediate appraisal of the situation and though treated for an unexplained injury to the nether regions, Mims appeared relatively unscathed. There's even talk he might make a run for the U.S. Congress. Most voters agree that he has the libido for the job. Miss LaBoom enjoyed a brief period of success when the Club Silicone Valley, where she was employed, billed her as "Lockjaw" LaBoom.

So, things were suspiciously normal in Edsel County. Katie and the Sergeant-major were back to being their old selves; the usual crowd was back at the bar; Z.Z was doing his best imitation of a drop-out, expatriate stock broker for the edification of the lovelies and I was just living day-to-day.

Peace comes at last to Edsel County. Right? Guess again! Whoever made up that sayin' about the calm before the storm knew what he was talking about.

thirty one

"Wherein an unwelcome visitor comes a knockin'..."

"Now here's the latest on Tropical Storm Kevin...".

We were all sitting around the bar at Katie's waiting on the latest update on a disturbance just east of the Virgin Islands and making the usual crude comments about the sexual proclivities of the storms. Male or female by name, the storms were always subjected to rude conjecture as to their results. One of the most popular jibes was aimed at Key West, "Let the damned storm go there! It's the only island that'll blow back!" This always led to a round of guffaws and some effort to update the jokes to fit the current storm.

"If Kevin does the Virgins, they'll still be Virgins when he leaves!" was about the level of the talk.

"Kevin is expected to reach hurricane strength by morning and pose a grave threat to the Virgin Islands and Puerto Rico. The current track to the west-northwest is expected to continue and little change is expected for the next forty-eight hours."

Much of the banter was hiding the concern felt by the assorted crew at the bar. Many made their living on or near the water and anything that stirred the status quo was basically money out of their pockets. So, while the joking continued, nearly all were thinking in the back of their minds, "Lord, let that thing just ease on out to sea and leave Edsel County alone." It had been years since anything more than a heavy breeze had disturbed the waters of the county and though the old-timers knew the potential for disaster, it was the newcomers, not realizing the power of a tropical cyclone, that were most at risk. Edsel County, like all the rest of south Florida had been subjected to overwhelming development resulting in trailer parks, shoddily built homes and strip malls. Most awaited their first exposure to anything approaching hurricane strength winds.

Z.Z. took a pull on his drink and said, "Bubba, where do you figure we oughta go if this thing looks like it might jump on us?"

I told him that I figured that unless the old boy got real serious, like over a hundred miles per hour, we'd do just as well to sit tight seeing as how both our houses had been around longer than we had and looked to be here after we were gone. We had shutters and just enough elevation to avoid anything other than a really big-time storm surge.

"We've got about thirty-six hours or so to watch what's happening then make a decision."

"Yeah. Katie...two more."

The next afternoon found us on the same two stools at Katie's with a little better attention being paid to the TV.

"Hurricane Kevin, with winds now approaching ninety miles per hour remains on a steady west-northwest track at thirteen miles per hour and poses a definite threat to the southeastern coast of Florida including Dade, Edsel and Monroe counties..."

"Damn ol' storm is tracking like it was on rails, Bubba. Lemme see, it's Tuesday so I figure it's gonna really screw up Friday's happy hour. Right?"

Leave it to Z.Z. to trivialize potential disaster.

"If that thing keeps on coming, it's gonna screw up a lot more than happy hour. They don't predict any further strengthening but it's already bad enough to kick butt around here." I was about through joking about Kevin. It was time to get serious.

"What say we head over to the supermarket and pick up a few items just ahead of the rush. It'll be a real zoo tomorrow."

"OK Bubba. How many cases of Manatee Malt you figger we need?" I pulled his hat over his face to shut him up. I guess he'll never learn...or will he?

thirty two

"Wherein Kevin pays a visit..."

"Hurricane warnings have been posted from Marathon in the Florida Keys north to Cape Canaveral. Kevin remains on a west-northwesterly course after raking the Leeward Islands and Hispaniola with one-hundred mile per hour winds and up to ten inches of rain. If the storm remains on its present course, it is expected to make landfall tomorrow afternoon somewhere south of Miami. Edsel County authorities have ordered the immediate evacuation of low-lying areas and trailer parks..."

"Hell, Bubba, that means the whole damned county. We're just one big trailer park 'bout knee-high above high tide."

We were taking a break from helping Katie and the Sergeant Major board up the restaurant for the rapidly approaching storm. We had already made our own preparations and stocked Z.Z.'s place with water and canned goods and, of course, a week's supply of Manatee Malt and a hundred pound block of ice. The decision was to stay at Z.Z.'s place as we had computed his elevation to be about six inches above mine. Every little bit helps we figured. Natasha Sue and Melanie had already moved in as both lived in places on the oceanside that would definitely bear the brunt of the storm. We had tried to persuade them to head over to the west coast but they said if we were going to stay, so would they.

"Boys, I reckon that about does it. Nothing left to do but lock the back door and board it over." Katie clicked off the TV set over the bar so Z.Z. and I took a last swallow of malt and followed her toward the back. "Bubba, here's a key to the door just in case we can't get back for a day or two after the storm. Might as well help yourself to whatever's here if the power's gonna be off for a while."

"Thanks, Katie. We'll look after things for you."

She patted us both on the rump as we went out the door and told her husband to nail the last piece of plywood in place. There was no place else to go now so we headed for home.

By the next morning, the wind had risen to a steady gale and the rain was starting to come in horizontal sheets. Every now and then, the lights would flicker and we wondered when we'd lose them for the duration. The satellite TV was working so we left it on the weather channel to see what was going on outside. Around noon, Natasha Sue first noticed a familiar background during one of the live reports from the area.

"Hoo boy!" she exclaimed. "We're in a world of trouble now! That ol' gal is reporting from Katie's parking lot."

We knew what she meant. When the weather folks showed up in your area, you could be pretty sure the storm wasn't far behind. It was sort of like answering a knock on your door and there's a guy there that says, "Hi. We're from Sixty Minutes!" Not a good omen.

"Wonder if they know they're on one of the lowest spots around here?" Z.Z. mused more or less to himself. "She's gonna be knee-deep soon."

Z.Z had a point. Katie's parking lot was lower than most of the surrounding area and for that reason, the building was raised a good eight or ten feet above it. Sure enough, by mid-afternoon, you could see that some serious flooding was taking place and it was evident that the eye of the storm was likely to pass directly over us by nightfall.

As the storm got closer, the noise level made by the wind and rain almost drowned out the TV's sound but we heard, "We have lost contact with our crew down in Edsel County, Florida since they reported by sat-phone they were having trouble finding a way to higher ground. We'll continue our efforts to establish contact and hope they're okay."

"Bubba, those folks just might be in a bit of trouble over there. If they didn't get out before the water rose much above where we saw it earlier, they're still there. The only place to go is Katie's porch and while I expect it'll stay above high water, it ain't gonna be very pleasant there as that porch is on the windward side."

Z.Z. had a point; though they would be above the flood, they would be exposed to the full force of the wind and rain and possible debris torn loose by the storm.

"Well, let's just hope they got the hell outta there in time. Katie's porch is a great place for happy hour but not this Friday afternoon!" I really didn't want to consider that someone was out in this mess.

"Maybe I just oughta sneak over there and make sure everything's copacetic. Folks just might appreciate a little company 'bout now."

"Are you nuts?" Melanie spoke first but was followed immediately by Natasha Sue, "Clyde Ryder, you're not going anywhere so forget it! Besides, there's no way to get there!"

I was about to second that statement but Z.Z was already slipping into his foul-weather gear and grinning.

"Well, I figure that if Grumpy Smith's ol' swamp buggy over there next door can make it through six feet of

Everglades muck, it can damn sure handle some good clean seawater. Noisy ol' thing's got eight-foot tires on it and the seat's ten feet above the ground. "Bout time it was good for something besides belchin' smoke and slingin' mud all over. Bubba, hand me that little radio over there."

He was referring to one of those hand-held marine band radios not much bigger than a can of sardines.

"..and look in that drawer there and let's see if that other one still works."

I rummaged through the drawer and found a beat-up mate to the one Z.Z. was now testing. Turning it on, I heard the reassuring clicks as Z.Z. keyed his transmitter.

"Okay, Bubba, looks like we're in business. Close that back door behind me. I'll call you as soon as I get the buggy started."

Just like St. Nick, with a wink he was gone.

thirty three

"Wherein an unlikely hero emerges..."

A week later, sitting in Katie's, Z.Z. is retelling the story for the umpteenth time for some reporters. But, I'm getting ahead of myself and anyway, it's Z.Z.'s story so I'll let him tell it:

"The way I figured it, those weather folks had to be one of two places: either on top of the truck or on Katie's porch; neither one which was gonna be real comfortable for the next few hours. It looked like Kevin was still a couple of hours from giving us his best shot so I'd better get with the program. A swamp buggy'll go through most anything short of a lava flow so I just borrowed Grumpy's and took off. If it hadn't been for the seat belt, I'da probably been blown off a couple of times when a real bad gust hit but that ol' buggy kept on chuggin'.

As I got close to Katie's here, I could just make out the truck which was covered up by a big gumbo limbo tree that was layin' across it. There was no way to tell if anybody was inside but the water was up to the window level so I sure hoped not. Anyway, I made a pass around the back here and as I came to the front, sure enough, there's the crew crouched down on the porch holding on to a corner post. At this point, I guess the water was about six feet or so deep; anyway it was lapping at the floor of the porch and there was no way to get to the roof. Not that anybody wanted to be up there.

I don't think they even knew I was there until I was twenty feet away. As noisy as that buggy was, the wind was louder. Kinda of like lying on the railroad tracks letting the train pass over you; not that I ever did that.

Well, I drove that buggy under the porch until the seats were right up against it and motioned for them to crawl aboard. That didn't take much coaxing and soon we were headed for high ground. Somehow the radio got lost in the shuffle so I couldn't report back to HQ that we were on our way in.

We were close to home when the eye passed over us so I knew we had thirty minutes or so of calm before all hell broke loose again. That last quarter mile turned out to be a pleasant drive. That was it 'cept for the back slappin' and high-fivin' when we got back to my place."

That's much the way Z.Z. tells the story every time; leaving out some of the more pertinent details. I guess I'll fill in the blanks.

True to his word, Z.Z. had checked in to say the buggy ran fine and he was on his way. He said there was no way to answer him as we couldn't be heard over the storm so he would just report in the blind. He continued to give us progress reports including the sighting of the tree-enveloped truck and finding the two people clinging to the porch. That was the last we heard from him until we heard the buggy coming during the lull in the storm.

He fails to mention in his public version how he was almost knocked unconscious by a broken tree limb that swept over him before he reached Katie's or how he got off the buggy to attempt to search the truck for the crew; wading in shoulder-deep water to peer in the cab. Lastly, he fails to mention that just as the female crew member released her hold on the corner post to board the buggy, a powerful gust slid her off the porch into the deep water where she could hardly stay afloat in her bulky gear. According to the other member of the crew, Z.Z. immediately jumped in after her and pulled her aboard the buggy; all the while bleeding at the temple where the limb struck him. That's when he lost the radio and couldn't report his success or the fact that he was okay.

Interestingly enough, when we surveyed the damage the next day, the only thing left of the porch was the corner posts. It's presumed it was carried away within minutes of Z.Z.'s timely rescue.

So, Edsel County is in a mop-up mode now. There were no deaths blamed on the storm and only a few minor injuries, Z.Z.'s among them. The weather people and others of the various media have given Z.Z. the "Attaboys" he richly deserves. The weather lady (person) even wears a small gold pin with the letters Z.Z. on it when she's on the air to remind folks of his deeds.

Leave it to our hero to find a downside to all this; he decided we could make a small fortune clearing the downed trees and brush and cutting it up for firewood. That is until he made a startling discovery:

"Bubba, I don't know of one damned fireplace in Edsel County!"

thirty four

"Wherein the good citizens hold a celebration..."

Aside from the loss of the porch, Katie's place came through relatively unscathed as did most of the county. Despite the high wind and water, there was not sufficient damage for the county to be declared a disaster area; at least, no more than it already was. Actually, the storm sorta cleared out some of the dead or dying vegetation resulting in a kind of cleanup, if you'll look at the bright side.

Surprisingly enough, our power company did a great job and things were back to normal in a day or so. We didn't have more than two or three blackouts a night. Seems that if lightning flashes anywhere within two-hundred miles, that's it for an hour or two. Go figure.

Like I said, Katie's was in pretty good shape and open for business within forty-eight hours. The insurance company had already settled on the loss of the porch; a settlement made easy owing to the fact that the insurance adjuster, Ed

"Doomsday" Dugan, was missing his daily respite from the rigors of insuring life and limb from fate's misfortunes. In other words, he was unhappy as hell that happy hour wasn't happening. He was not alone.

It was the following Friday's happy hour, when, at the bar, someone suggested that a celebration might be in order to thank the powers that be for sparing us from a crueler fate. Amidst the hubbub, Katie's voice rose with a suggestion;

'Let's do a pig!"

Now, to the uninitiated, that can have a lot of meanings; ranging from the 60's, "Kill a cop!" to some form of bestiality best not pursued further here. What Katie meant was to get a big, whole hog and cook that sucker over open coals for hours on end until we fall upon it in a southern ritual called a "Pig Pick".

First, this involves the digging of a rather large pit in someone's yard or other appropriate location; in this case, Katie's parking lot. Fortunately, "Shaky" Simpson from the county road department happened to have a jackhammer on his truck and the pit only took a matter of moments to carve out of the coquina stone that was the base of Katie's lot. While Shaky was doing his thing, Z.Z. and the Sargent Major lit out for Aboud's Pig Farm over by the turnpike. Ol' Aboud usually has several pigs ready for the fire or he can dress one out before you can say, "It'll never pass for chicken!"

By the time Z.Z. and the Major got back with the pig, we'd gotten some charcoal going in the pit and soon it was time to commence. Now this is not like throwing a steak on the grill for five minutes or barbecuing some chicken for a while; this is a slooooow process. When we got the pig settled over the coals, it was approaching midnight; just about right for a great party the next evening.

Yep. Cooking a pig like this takes the better part of a night and day. That's why you start around midnight planning to eat eighteen hours later. Now the hard part of this slow-cooking process is that someone has to add a few coals to the fire every now and then. You don't just build a fire and throw the pig on it. Therefore, keeping someone awake to feed the fire is the most difficult step in a successful pig roast. Especially when the cooks have been toasting the carcass, themselves and anything else they can use for an excuse to have another drink.

Usually, the wives, girlfriends or other observers have, by the time the cooking actually starts, figured that reservations for tomorrow night at Tampico Tony's Taco Heaven just down the road might be good insurance. Oh, ye of little faith.

Natasha and Melanie opted out of the ritual dancing and traditional mantra chanting in favor of a night's sleep which didn't really bother me and Z.Z. We happily joined our comrades in praise of our ceremonial icons; Barf, Snnzzz, and Sooeeeey!

If Aurora, goddess of the Dawn had, upon her coming, viewed the scene in Katie's parking lot, our sad company would have joined her unfortunate husband as a grasshopper. A sorrier lot was not to be found in Edsel County that morning.

The one advantage to waking up in the steel bed of a pickup truck without benefit of pillows or other bedclothes is the certainty that the day can only get better. Once you've gotten over the crick in your neck and refreshed your breath with a Manatee Malt, you're ready to face another day. I failed to mention that when I awoke, said pickup truck was lurching down the road with a semi-conscious Z.Z. at the wheel. I suffered in silence until he dropped me at my place whereupon I thanked him and dismissed him with a weak dry heave promising to still be alive come evening.

Breakfast: Alka-Seltzer
Mid-morning snack: Screwdriver
Lunch: Bloody Mary (see-through variety)
High tea: Red eye (Manatee Malt with Bloody Mary mix)
Cocktails: Straight Manatee Malt

Let the festivities begin!

Fortunately for the pig and for those anticipating the Saturday night festivities, Pepe Figuroa and his firemen had, in contradiction to their sworn duty, maintained the cooking fire throughout the night thereby insuring the pig's readiness by evening.

Thus is was that evening found us once again in Katie's parking lot in high good spirits. Natasha and Melanie were somewhat concerned about the rather ashen appearance of Z.Z. and myself but we assured them we were of sufficient health to enjoy the evening. The good Doctor Jose Cuervo had been kind enough to prescribe a rapid cure for what ailed us and we assured them of a gala evening ahead. Needless to say, the two girls were as much the center of attention as the savory porker on the grill.

Natasha was in old-style Capri pants with an off the shoulder Bolero top which made her look about thirty-five years old going on sixteen. Melanie was in what was purported to be a linen shift but looked more like a layer of gauze; a thin layer of gauze under which was very little in the way of lingerie. The overall effect was startling for a librarian, especially when she stepped in front of a strong light. Every time one or the other stood up, you could hear a sharp intake of breath followed by the dull "oomph" of some husband being poked in the ribs by an alert wife.

After much pre-dinner fellowship, Katie announced that it was time for dinner and that before tearing into the pig, she thought it proper that we all give thanks for our good fortune. Thus, she had invited the Reverend Kareem Saul O'Connor to offer the blessing over this event. There was some controversy over having a Kareem Saul bless a pig but it was outweighed by the O'Connor surname; the rationale being that any good Irishman would be more than happy to do so. The ecumenical significance would be lost on the crowd anyway. On Sunday mornings, most of them could be found out on the reef fishing or diving where communion consisted of Manatee Malt and Fritos. I mean, these people know where Heaven is!

Anyhow, after a shalom or two, a few allah akbars, and a whole bunch of avés, someone hollered, "Amen, for God's sake!" and we went down on that pig. That sweet pork was just falling off the bone and all you had to do was grab a handful and get at it. There was cole slaw, baked beans, biscuits and hush puppies and gallons of good old sweetened, iced tea. Z.Z says the only way he could ever give up drinking would be to have an unlimited supply of barbecue and iced tea. Folks are always saying scotch is an acquired taste; well, I believe a man is born with a taste for barbecued pork and iced tea. A southern man anyway.

Now any party like this is certain not to go unnoticed by politicians who have a nose for convivial gatherings of more than four voters and this was not to be an exception. Sheriff Sam took the stump and briefly declared his appreciation to the county citizens for their cooperation and help during and after the storm and asked that he be remembered at election time.

Next up came Commissioner Sanford Mims, remember him? Sure enough, he launched into a tirade against all the things that were going awry in Washington and vowed to change the way business was done in our nation's capital. Thus did the Honorable Commissioner Sims announce his candidacy for Congress. Mrs. Sims, knowing the political tides were running in her husband's favor, stood at his side, beaming, secure in the knowledge that she had the old boy by the short and curlies because as she had recently told him, "One more bounce with Bambi and your political career goes La Boom!"

The general consensus among the crowd seemed to be that now Mims could spread his modest larceny throughout the entire district instead of just fleecing the good people of Edsel County.

Half the crowd was asleep by the time Mims finished his oratory. Sated on the rich dinner, everybody was too tired to fight or otherwise create a ruckus and only a few half-hearted younger folks tried to dance to the rock band, Semi-hole and the Half-Assed Indians.

Even Z.Z. was pooped and he and Natasha bid us good night and we all headed for home. I was barely awake when Melanie asked me "Bubba, did you ever want to be a movie star?" I think she hit me when I mumbled "Only if it involves Linda Lovelace."

thirty five

"Wherein the arts come to Edsel County..."

It was several days before the significance of Melanie's question about the movies hit me. Several of us were passing the time in Katie's debating the merits of NAFTA, GAT and other items of national interest including how the current scandal involving the chairman of the Senate Foreign Relations Committee and two female sumo wrestlers would effect our trade deficit with Japan. The general consensus was that most folks were laughing too hard to worry one way or another. The cover photos on all the tabloids told the story; the ecstatic face of the good senator peeking from between two mountains of flesh or maybe it was four mountains of flesh, had the presses running overtime. Press aides insist that this was on the senator's itinerary as a, "...cultural event in which classic sumo moves are demonstrated". Capitol Hill wags have dubbed it the "Hump the Honda" episode.

Anyway, things were pretty slow when Katie sidles over and says, "Don't look now but that's Manny "The Frog" Fogelman sittin' over there by the fish tank." Of course, we all turned as one and looked and, sure enough, there's this rotund guy who's about five-foot-two with big aviator sunglasses on and little ears that lay back against his head. It wasn't hard to see how Manny got his nickname. What Katie failed to mention was the presence at the same table of just about the hottest young, nubile bimb..., uh star, to come out of Hollywood in at least a week. Yep, right there in Katie's was Miss Dorothy Comings, in the flesh, of which there was a sufficiency in all the right places. Swearing that her name was indeed her own, the studio had capitalized on the current trend and she was now known as Dot Com. Their reasoning being that people heard that phrase about ten zillion times a day and it had to be good for the box office.

So, our erudite group began to question the presence of so hallowed a star in our midst; something like this: "Oh God! Katie, I'll give you twenty-five dollars for that chair when she leaves!" or "I'll bet if you go over to the other side of the fish tank and look thru, her bazooms will be twice as big!" Finally, Z.Z., of all people, got to the crux of the deal "Why?"

"They're here to shoot some scenes for a film they're doing. Supposed to be around for two or three weeks, I heard." Katie shed some light on the situation. "They'll be hiring some locals for small parts and extras in the next few days and may even shoot some stuff here. I didn't want to get everybody stirred up 'til it was happening."

The notion that Dot Com would be in our midst for the foreseeable future set off a round of speculation as to where she was staying and how she could best spend her hours away from the cameras. The more conservative ideas involved nude sunbathing on Dildo Key. (A real place; look it up!)

Putting two and two together, Melanie's question about movies, a noticeable drop in her ardor and the presence of the Hollywood types added up to only one thing; she had a new passion. To become a star! It soon became obvious that she was not alone. Half the county's population suddenly went Hollywood. There wasn't a pair of sunglasses to be found in the stores and even the gals at the post office had on enough make-up to put Tammy Faye to shame.

Needless to say, the most garish of the entire lot was none other than...need I say? Yep...ol' Z.Z.! The master of tackiness had climbed to new heights. Stay with me now! The lizard skin boat shoes were still with us but did absolutely nothing for the riding breeches, bush jacket, ascot and beret that topped them.

Suspended around his neck by a piece of monofilament leader from his tackle box was an old 35mm lens that he picked up at "Hock me! Hock me!" pawn shop. This he would peer through and make weird humming sounds punctuated by, "Close up! Two shot! Print it!" and like terms.

More seriously, Melanie had apparently been discovered, tested and cast in some relatively important part much to the consternation of Candy Jr. who had publicly refused to kiss the "Frog" stating that, "...ol' Walt himself couldn't turn that one into a prince and I'm not about to try."

Thus it was that Melanie was in the movies, Candy Jr. was in a major funk and Z.Z. was *non compos mentis*.

What I failed to mention was that I'd been retained as an assistant to the location scout, Rita Romero, after running into her one day at Katie's. Rita had tried acting but decided she'd "...rather do it for fun than for business." This meant that the two of us spent most of the day running around the county looking for authentic Florida keys atmosphere. We always ended up back at Katie's where Rita smoothed up her notes and reviewed the day's Polaroids. She took dozens of pictures when she thought a site might be suitable for a scene and occasionally had me take some shots of her, "...for her scrapbook", she said. It was the third day of shooting palm trees and pelicans when Rita handed me the camera and quicker than you could say, "Victoria's Secret", had shucked her jeans, tee-shirt and what used to be call unmentionables but was now mostly unseeables and the next thing I knew, I had a pocketful of pictures of Rita in the raw. I figured that scrapbook would be worth a look sometime.

On the way back to Katie's from that shoot, she informed me that she liked to post new stuff up on one of those websites dedicated to what she called an "alternative lifestyle" which I knew meant that not too many good ol' boys would be loggin' on that one. Seemed like a shame though 'cause she was one fine looking gal and had the smarts to go with it. Turned out that it was just as well we didn't have to do the mating dance thing because I sorta, as we say, got a better deal.

thirty six

"Wherein our intrepid sidekick weighs in..."

Damn! Now I gotta take up the slack for Bubba again because he's fallen into the manure pit and come out smelling like one of them designer after-shaves. Well, maybe better than that!

We've had movie people crawling all over Edsel County for nearly a month. I mean, you can't get a thing done 'cause everybody is fallin' all over themselves tryin' to be a star. I wasn't all that interested myself and just sorta sat back and watched the dogfight over who could be the most star-struck. Ol' Melanie scored herself a deal right off and that was the end of her affair with poor ol' Bubba. Candy Jr. was in a real huff because the best she could do was the second unit director who kept going off into the boondocks to shoot background footage. Of course, he sometimes had some real interesting stuff to show at the dailies. The crew loved his work and Candy Jr's.

I decided the best thing to do was just hang out at Katie's and take'em as they come. It's amazin' what you can do with a clipboard and an attitude. About one in every five or six of the aspiring lovelies hereabouts was willin' to do a more lengthy interview with a casting director (me, in case you didn't figger that out already) and that's the closest I ever came to shootin' fish in a barrel. Maybe we'd better just skip over that part and get to the rest of the story.

For reasons that defy all sorta logic, Bubba got hired on for a few days as a location scout, but that's not what I'm talking about. It seems that Dot Com spotted him one day while he was on the set advising "The Frog" on something or other and overheard them talking about Dildo Key. Like any red-blooded young Hollywood starlet, this drew her attention and she inquired as to the nature of the conversation.

Everybody around here knows that Dildo Key is down in Florida Bay a little ways and ain't nothin' more than a mangrove-covered sandbar about five-hundred yards in diameter. 'Course, when we were young, Bubba insisted that a dildo key was how my Aunt Eugenia gained access to her bedside table and we searched for it a lot of times with no success. Probably just as well.

Anyhow, Bubba wound up taking Miss Dot Com over there in the boat, OUR boat, I should mention, and the rest, as they say, is history. I'm not real sure how he does it and he's not real willing to share his secret with his best friend of some thirty-five years but you have to give him credit; he always comes back from his adventures smiling. (Dangled that partacycle, didn't I?) So now Bubba is hangin' out in Dot Com's trailer and Manny the Frog is overjoyed with the whole arrangement. Seems that Miss Com is notorious for showin' up late, blowin' lines and stuff like that. Now that Bubba is "available" on the set between takes, she's rippin' through the script like she wrote it so she can get back to the trailer and "relax". Manny's ahead of schedule and under budget which makes him one happy picnicker. You're not likely to see Bubba's name when they roll the credits though. I don't think they got a category for what he's doing unless it's that "key grip" thing.

So now, Melanie is in a snit though she'd already bailed out, Candy Jr. is dumbfounded by whatever it is that Dot's got that she doesn't and Bubba is in tall cotton. I've discovered some amazing talent hereabouts and hate to have to disappoint them but Natasha is due back from her newspaper assignment up in Miami in the next couple of days so I guess I'll have to retire from this casting thing even though it has its advantages.

Maybe I'd better go ride my bicycle into the brush a couple of times; best way to explain the scratches. I wonder if anybody ever got a hickey fallin' off a bike? It'll just have to be a first!

"Cut! Print! Put your clothes on!" Damn! This movie business is a hoot!

thirty seven

"Wherein normalcy (?) returns to Edsel County..."

Whew! That movie making sure does tax a fellow's stamina. Well, I wasn't exactly involved in the actual filming process. Let's just say that I sorta acted as morale consultant to the movie's female star. You know how it is with those actresses; being high strung and all. Takes a lot of TLC to keep them calmed down so they can work. Anyway, "It's a wrap!" as they say in the business and Manny and company have lit out for the left coast.

I guess cooking and eating three big meals a day will put the weight back on me soon and my jeans won't be trying to slide to my knees. Speaking of knees, they've pretty much healed now.

Z.Z. is in the doghouse again since trying to convince Natasha Sue that a hickey on his shoulder was caused by a fall off his bike into a gumbo limbo thicket. "Be the first damned gumbo limbo with teeth!" sums up her attitude. This too shall pass as the saying goes but it'll take a few weeks of soft soap on his part to thaw her out.

Oh, one other movie thing. Manny says he'll have the world premier right here at the Edsel County Drive-In and Skeet Range. It'll be six months or so before he finishes editing and so on but that'll give us time to prepare for a major blowout. Z.Z.'s hoping that Joe Bob Briggs will show up and add a little class to the festivities.

Sheriff Sam has had his hands full trying to get rid of a cult of what he call "toad-lickers" that had been camped out in a mangrove thicket on the gulf side of the county. Seems like there was a dozen or so over-the-hill hippies that were trapping every bufo toad they could find and then they'd hold a licking ceremony.

From what I can gather, that old bufo toad has got something that puts peyote mushrooms to shame. Whatever it is has been said to kill dogs that picked one up in their mouth. Anyhow, those folks would hold their licking and then run around in circles, tearing each others clothes off and howling at the moon. Z.Z. allowed as how that was mostly normal for some folks around here but Sheriff Sam said it went against good order and discipline so he chased them off in the direction of Key West. "Let'em go down there and lick whatever they like," he said. "Nobody'll know the difference."

Our county commissioners are planning a ceremony honoring the sheriff and Chief Figuroa and the fire department for their actions during the hurricane and rumor has it that Z.Z is to be included on the list of honorees. That's for his rescue of those weather folks and I gotta say that I'm glad the commission saw fit to include him. He deserves it if anybody does. There's to be bonuses for the county folks and some sorta cash award to Z.Z. which means a windfall for Katie's as that's exactly where it'll go. Of course, all the regulars there will share in the wealth as Z.Z. just loves playing host the few times he can afford it. And, I suspect the recognition might just help to soften Natasha up a little bit. Even though she's supposed to be the hard-bitten, objective newspaper type, she's got a big old soft heart for something like this. She might even lay a little reward on him herself. Let's hope so.

thirty eight

"Wherein a temporary peace settles over Edsel County..."

Well, quicker than Z.Z. could say, "Enough of cloning them sheep, those ol' boys oughta work on a Faith Hill or two!"; we found out that Billy Ray Muckenfuss is bringing his road show to the Edsel County Memorial Auditorium and Sons of the Confederacy armory. This is sure to be the high point of our social season and a show to end all shows. The opening act is Moonshine Mustafa and the Palestine Plowboys; fresh from a long-running engagement at Beirut's Howitzer Plaza Hotel. The only problem with these guys is their volume; someone said they couldn't hear each other real well but every time the drummer pedaled his bass a little too hard, they all dove for cover. They can't be as bad as last month's featured attraction, Thelonious Assault; four guitars and a drummer and a bunch of speakers about the size of the Taj Mahal. I heard that some fish out in the bay are still swimming in circles from the low frequency sounds put out by this band. Word is that some of those Greenpeace folks are blaming them for a whale beaching in Madagascar.

Candy Jr. has dropped by a couple of times to offer her services as a hospitality hostess for our visitors and I figure this might just be my chance to witness a free-for-all that the county won't soon forget. Not that I countenance the kind of rowdy behavior that is certain to result from a meeting between Candy Jr. and Billy Ray's entourage. On the other hand, I figure we might get a better feel for the term "synergy" when these two forces come together and create some sorta new party animal. Z.Z. has made me promise that I'll introduce him to Billy Ray and drag him along to any parties that I get wind of. I know this is pouring oil on the fire but, what the hell, if he survives, it'll be sure to calm him down for a week or two while he recovers.

Speaking of Z.Z., word is that he has been nominated for a National Lifesaving Medal and a trip to Washington, as in D.C., is in the works for next month. He says I can go with him because Natasha Sue is scheduled to be off on another newspaper assignment then.

"Bubba, you reckon we can get into the Oral Office for a little while with a couple of those internals?" Ever the optimist!

While I'm on the subject of my old buddy, he told me that he stopped in the Malelucca Lounge the other Wednesday night for a quick one and the place was about the same as it's been for a few years now. You see, the Malelucca used to be about the only other watering hole besides Katie's that we patronized. That is, until the median age of the women that frequented the place began to creep toward social security eligibility. A few of the local wags even began to refer to it as "Menopause Manor". Don't get me wrong; it wasn't quite the blue-hair crowd but a lot of these DWIs (That's as in what happened to their husbands; Divorced, Widowed or Institutionalized) drove Buicks and Grand Marquis which gives you an idea of what I'm talking about.

Anyhow, Z.Z. says he forgot it was singles night also known as "Grab a Granny" night and, sure enough, the bar was full of women; half of 'em wrapped in sweaters and the other half fanning up a breeze that made it hard to light a cigarette.

"There was a new Jag in the parking lot but I found out it belonged to this little bitty old gal who looked like she was the sole support of three or four of them Palm Beach plastic surgeons. One old gal hit on me but I didn't go for her. I wouldn't say she was a dog but I swear that when I saw her drive away, she had her head out the window."

He summed the place up when he said, "Bubba, it's a sight to behold. There's enough nail polish on those old gals to paint a semi and you could stucco a house with the make-up they wear." The boy does have a colorful way with words, don't you think?

I guess we'll leave the "Manor" off our tour itinerary for the foreseeable future. Katie's is more our style and every now and then some unsuspecting young lovely wanders in and for whoever gets lucky, it's kinda like finding a prize in a jelly donut. Unexpected but a pleasant suprise just the same.

Anyhow, I'm anxious to see if this Washington thing comes off as advertised. My aims are set a little higher than Z.Z.'s when it comes down to sightseeing up there. I can't wait to visit Abe and the Smithsonian but Z.Z. is more of a mind to see "...where that ol' gal, Fannie, and Wilbur frolicked in the pool and the steps where Ol' Whatsisname, that congressman from South Carolina, got tootled."

I suppose we'll compromise and just go watch'em print money. There can't be too much harm in that.

thirty nine

"Wherein politicians and pigs prevail..."

Have you ever been to the "seat" of our guvmint? Well, Z.Z. and I just got back from our trip to the nation's capital and, let me tell you, one trip is enough unless you've been elected to go up there and fatten up at the public trough. Now don't get me wrong, we saw some sights that nearly brought tears to this ol' boy's eyes. Standing at Abe's feet and thinking what this nation's been through was one of those deals that makes the hair stand up on the back of your neck.

And my buddy Z.Z., for all his hoopla about what he wanted to see, calmed down when we went to the Vietnam wall. You see, his Uncle Daryl was one of the early casualties before that mess became "official" and they started keepin' score. Besides, Daryl was a civilian workin' for some shadow outfit and so he wouldn't have made the wall on any count. Z.Z. says about the time Daryl got killed, there was probably only a dozen or so casualties and that's about the time somebody should of figured it was time to get outta Dodge City.

Anyhow, we got to see the sights and Z.Z., who got his medal without incident, managed to thank everyone without tripping over his tongue although he almost lost it when he spotted the Undersecretary of Something-Or-Other sitting in the front row crossing and uncrossing her legs in a most unlady-like manner. He allowed as how he was one taxpayer gettin' his money's worth.

Oh yeah. I almost forgot; we did hit the Senate gallery for a bit and that was a major disappointment. We figured we'd listen in for a bit on the law-making process but the place was empty except for some old guy propped up against the lectern mumbling so's you couldn't understand him. One of the guards said he was the distinguished one-hundred-and-one-year old senator from South Carolina who had his speeches filmed when the chamber was empty for later dubbing by a young newscaster from Monck's Corner. They were then cut into soundbites for broadcast in his home state. Z.Z. said he wondered what the fellow dubbing the speech did about the snores.

That and a drive by the White House wrapped up the trip for us. I didn't want to take a tour of the executive mansion with Z.Z. because I figured he'd get us in trouble quicker than you could say, "That dress isn't you. I'd get rid of it!" Then we thought we saw some of those folks from down in Aiken, you know the ones that were outside the gate when we got there with the nuke stuff? They were camped out across the street in a place called Lafayette Park and didn't look like they'd cleaned up much since then.

So, it was time to get on home and get ready for the big concert with Billy Ray and all. This was gonna require some preparation, mainly getting our livers in shape.

Unfortunately, while eating breakfast in some place just off I-95 around Rocky Mount, I happened to pick up the local paper and see that a major event was taking place just up the road in Hillsborough. We've already discussed our propensity for cultural events heavy with local flavor and Hillsborough's "Hog Day" sure seemed to be right up our alley. I mean it's not every day that you get to combine hogs and history. We decided to check it out.

Like so many places, this little town had started something that was getting out of hand. It's bad enough when the population triples on a Saturday but when they all bring dressed pigs, it's a mess. Naw, I don't mean pigs that have been dressed out as in slaughtered; I'm talking about pigs that are dressed up---in clothes!

Did you ever see a Poland China pig in a tuxedo? A Vietnamese pot-bellied pig in a grass skirt? A sow in a shift? Well, maybe that one at the VFW dance on a Saturday night. Pigs of all shapes and sizes in every imaginable costume. Three little pigs, pigs in a blanket, the pig 'n whistle, you name it.

Needless to say, when "Dorothy" came by with the Cowardly Lion, the Tinman, and the Scarecrow, the day begin to take shape. "Dorothy" had pigtails, a little short skirt and red, sparkly spike heels of the "catch me; you-know-what" variety. The three pigs were on leashes and I'll have to admit looked pretty good in their costumes.

Being the gentlemanly sort, we spoke kindly to her whereupon she said she was off to see the Wizard and did we want to come along? Well, we quickly established that I was somewhat of an accomplished pigman due to my time at the hog wash and we hit it right off.

Let me tell you, we made a day of it. We ate barbecue and drank beer 'til we couldn't move then hooted and danced 'til we could eat and drink some more. Along about dark, it started to rain and "Dorothy" said to run for her van which was just outside the park where they were having the party. Z.Z. and the pigs were wandering around somewhere lookin' for, as Z.Z. put it, "...a wicked witch." I figured the pigs had sense enough to get out of the rain so I took off after "Dorothy".

Sometime in the wee hours, after lots of "Oinks" and playin' "This little piggie...", I remembered that Z.Z. was somewhere out there on his own. Not a good thing. "Dorothy" woke up long enough to mix up her stories saying, "You huff and puff pretty good, Big Bad Wolf. Stop by next time you're on the Yellow Brick Interstate."

Most of the vendor's tents were down and gone but I found Z.Z and the three porkers sleeping peacefully under the beer tent. Z.Z. had apparently discovered a mother lode of a couple of overlooked kegs and, generous soul that he is, had filled one of the empty ice tubs with beer for the pigs and used the hose on the tap for himself. All four were piled comfortably together and Z.Z. looked quite content even maybe smiling a little under the fake pig snout that hid his nose. If there'd been a camera around, he would have had to keep me in Manatee Malt for the rest of my life lest the picture go public. Some of his less charitable friends might have remarked that it wasn't the first time but he won't hear it from me.

So, we were "pigged out" so to speak as we headed for the peace and quiet of home. Yeah, right!

forty

"Wherein a minor debacle foretells a major one..."

Some time back, I think I mentioned Z.Z.'s stubborn mindset against wearing socks. I'm not a real fan of them either as I believe they are necessary only for weddings and funerals, neither of which is mine, I hope. Z.Z., however, still insists that any wedding that takes place between Natasha Sue and him will be sockless on his part.

I mention this because I was thinking of the other day when several of us were sitting around Katie's discussing world affairs when somehow we got around to trying to figure out who was the last one of us to have on socks or, for that matter, long pants. You see, the unofficial Edsel County uniform is mostly boat shoes or plain sneakers, shorts with several pockets and tee-shirts. Belts are optional; suspenders are a no-no.

About the closest thing to a dress code that I know of is Katie's policy of no tank tops; at least not on three-hundred-pound Harley riders with armpits that look like those old boys on a box of Smith Brothers cough drops. Exceptions to the tank top rule usually involve young lovelies of the female persuasion, especially those qualifying for the C-cup follies. Local wags say that Katie should charge a cover when Candy Jr. comes in and sits down under one of the air-conditioning vents. Z.Z swears he can hear the fabric stretch. I know I can hear me and a bunch of others swallow hard.

Anyhow, the only one in the bunch that would own up to wearing long pants in the last month was Edsel County undertaker "Digger" Dunbar, owner of Dunbar's Mortuary, Mausoleum and Tuxedo Rental. I guess it sort of goes with the territory in his case. We didn't hold it against "Digger" as this instance was for a tourist's family and didn't really count against our principles. Besides, he swore he didn't have on socks; he just took some shoe polish and painted his ankles black to maintain some decorum.

As usual, it takes me a while to get to the matter at hand which is to relate to you the events of Billy Ray Muckenfuss' visit to Edsel County. Most of the participants have regained some measure of consciousness by now except maybe for our esteemed attorney, "Toe Jam" Jones who suffered a concussion while trying to sneak into his house after our after-concert party. This was, however, some eight hours after the concert was over, Toe Jam having fallen in the clutches of Billy's old girlfriend, "Veronica Velcro". I suppose I should have warned him when I saw him backstage talking trash to her. Sheriff Sam says it's a good thing Toe Jam's wife is cross-eyed or she might of hit him squarely and killed him. Everybody figures Toe Jam will have to toe the line for a while now and his wife was overheard at the supermarket the other day telling one of her girlfriends, "...and we'll see just how horny that little so-and-so is when he wakes up!" Lordy, lordy; you play, you pay!

But there I go getting ahead of the story as usual.

As you know, I'm in rather tight with Billy Ray and his entourage as a result of our best-selling records so everybody of more than a passing acquaintance was on my case to get them tickets, backstage passes and the like for the upcoming concert. Sometimes I think the problems of fame outweigh the perks but I have to admit that having Candy Jr. spend the better part of a Saturday night and Sunday morning persuading me to include her in the festivities was a definite upper. Go ahead and call me weak-willed; a man's gotta do what a man's gotta do!

Anyhow, the concert was held Friday night at the Edsel County Memorial Auditorium and Sons of the Confederacy armory which is only two roadkills south of Katie's so naturally the restaurant became headquarters for all concerned. Katie put up some temporary screens next to the fish tank to close off part of the restaurant so Billy Ray could enjoy a little privacy. It was a little disconcerting, however, to see the bug-eyed customers peering through the tank for a glimpse of the star.

The usual cast of characters accompanied Billy Ray on the tour. This included his wife, Rose, Veronica, Fat-Butt, Omar (and his cousin Zamfir who came down from Yeehaw Junction for the festivities) and the usual assortment of back-up musicians, singers, roadies, groupies and a couple of people that nobody seemed to know what it was they did. With two of those big land yachts and a like number of semis pulled up in Katie's parking lot, it was sorta like the circus had come to town; minus the elephants, of course. It certainly gave new meaning to the word "menagerie".

As Wednesday and Thursday were open dates, the entourage got in a day early meaning that the whole crowd had an extra day to get really bent out of shape. Billy Ray had expressed a desire to go deep-sea fishing so Z.Z. and I had engaged the services of local fishing legend, Captain Abraham "Ahab" Albury and his boat, the "Pea Pod". Thus it was on Thursday morning that a motley crew of hangovers and hangers-on set sail for the Gulf Stream to do battle with the unsuspecting fish.

The night before, Billy Ray had invited most everyone at Katie's within hearing to join the fishing party. Fortunately, the locals were aware that the weather wasn't conducive to a leisurely day at sea and passed on his hospitality. Others of us weren't so lucky. I told Z.Z. that the ocean was kicking up a good chop and we might just be better off hanging around in the back bay drinking beer. He allowed as how Billy Ray had expressed his desire to hook "...a really big'un." and wasn't going to be denied this opportunity. I never learn, remember?

In addition to Billy Ray, Veronica, a couple of the back-up girls and the odd musician or two, it was just me and Z.Z.; oh yeah, and Candy Jr.

From my earlier reporting, you might suspect that Billy Ray is not himself at the crack of dawn or at the crack of noon, for that matter. Anyhow, a couple of the guitar players got him onto the boat and settled him into a fishing chair and we headed out. The sun came up and soon Veronica and Candy Jr. began a contest to see who could show more skin. It was a case of "I'll see your warm-up jacket and raise you my cut-offs." until both were down to tee shirts and bikinis. Well, quicker than ol' Kenny could say, "...you gotta know when to hold'em and know when to fold'em!", Candy Jr. was out of the bikini bottom revealing one of those little ol' Brazilian string things and other assets. Veronica should have folded right there but she was game. She whipped off her shirt and her bikini top as if to say, "I'm betting the ranch!" but I knew it was over because Candy Jr. wasn't Cantaloup Queen for three years running without good cause. She looked at me and Z.Z. with a little smile and shucked the shirt. The string bottom had a string top! That fanny floss just went around her waist and then around her neck and that was that.

Well, as you know, I have been called upon to audit her assets from time to time but what genetics can do never fails to amaze me. I thought Z.Z.'s eyes were going to dry up 'cause I know he hadn't blinked for a full minute; even Veronica was staring 'til she gave a little bow acknowledging her defeat. That was when we went aground.

It seems Ahab and the mate had also been engrossed in the show and failed to note that we had drifted off course and run up on the only sandbar within miles. The sudden, jarring stop threw us all around and Candy Jr. landed in the chair on top of Billy Ray who must have been dreaming about fishing 'cause he woke up and started hollering, "I got a big'un, I got a big'un!" When he realized what the "big'un" was, he too could only stare in amazement until he passed out again.

I suggested to the girls that we might be better off if they covered some of their attractions, or in this case, their distractions. The crew was still focused on the girls' splendid display and seemed unaware of our predicament.

So, we passed the morning waiting for a tow boat to come pull us off the bar. Billy Ray remained in the chair, the girls had regained some degree of modesty and the rest of us sat around drinking our Manatee Malts and recalling the spectacle we had witnessed. Z.Z. summed up what the guys were thinking, "Bubba, it's just like on Gilligan's Island. Which one...Ginger or Mary Ann?"

Things would get better---for a while.

forty one

"Wherein an un-natural disaster is avoided--- for the most part..."

Once the tow boat freed us from the embarassing (or is that bare-assing) predicament and our intrepid captain returned us to the marina, Z.Z., Candy Jr., Veronica and I retired to Katie's for a bit of lunch. Z.Z. was keeping pretty quiet for once and I just figured he hadn't gotten over the shock of being in proximity to two, shall we say, rather well-proportioned young ladies. Not to say that Natasha Sue can't hold her own under most circumstances but this was big-league pulchritude while Natasha Sue was still in Triple-A.

He perked up considerably as we walked into Katie's though, taking Veronica's arm and crooking it through his so it looked like she was clinging to him. This struck me as a bad idea because I knew the word would get back to Natasha Sue and he'd be in deep doo-doo again. If you recall, I mentioned some time back that Veronica's nickname was "Velcro"; hold that thought! I'm not the only one that never learns.

Somewhere around dark, Katie offered to throw a bucket of cold water on the lot of us if we didn't take our gropings elsewhere, thus it was that Candy Jr. and I departed for my place leaving Z.Z. and Veronica to fend for themselves. For reasons of my own, I wasn't thinking about just what this evening might hold for ol' Z.Z. Hey, he's a big boy. At least, he thought he was.

That evening, as I was to learn later, the county suffered a major brown-out as the result of one of Billy Ray's roadies plugging in the umpteenth amp for a sound check. This overloaded the county's power grid and disabled every microwave oven around for a couple of hours. Disgruntled housewives nearly overloaded the telephone system to boot; how the hell were they expected to get Stouffer's on the table?

The next morning, after Candy Jr. had departed, I was sitting in the kitchen trying to get a grip on a cup of coffee when the phone rang.

"Bubba!" Z.Z was whispering. "You gotta help me. I'm at..." I heard the phone drop and a woman's voice, "Naughty boy, Clyde, naughty...!" Then a disconnect. There is no mistaking Veronica's husky drawl when she is in one of her "moods". I just giggled; whatever was happening to Ol' Clyde, I figured he deserved.

The day passed without further communication from my buddy and as showtime approached, he was still missing so Candy Jr. and I ventured backstage to wish Billy Ray well and enjoy some refreshments. Fatbutt offered us glasses of Chateau de Retch champagne and allowed as how this was gonna be a show for the ages. From experience, I knew this was probably true because Billy Ray was face down on the dressing table; his usual pre-performance position. I was a little surprised to see Veronica but she just smiled and nodded. She looked happy. Not a good sign.

As I would later learn, Veronica had indeed attached herself to the unfortunate Z.Z. and held him captive for nearly twenty-four hours. He managed to escape out a window while she was getting dressed for the Friday evening show.

He spent the next two days hiding out at his Cousin Lulubelle's, an unfortunate choice as she spent the entire time pumping him for information about Veronica's methods and practices in the event some hapless male wandered on to her property. He asked me if I thought we ought to alert the power company meter reader just in case and I told him that those ol' boys were pretty nimble from dodging Rottweilers, pit bulls and such and could probably evade Lulu's clutches.

Z.Z.'s escape and evasion meant he missed the show and other festivities. This also released Veronica on poor ol' Toe Jam who thought he'd died and gone to heaven for a brief period. She latched on to him right after the show and Toe Jam was grinning like a possum as Veronica started pulling him toward the stage door. As we would later learn, Veronica subjected him to much the same fate as Z.Z. except that Toe Jam managed to escape around dawn only to suffer a concussion at the hands of his wife. Out of the fire, into the frying pan, so to speak.

The concert itself was a flat-out winner. Billy Ray and the band played for a solid hour and a half before they took a break, then came back and did another two hours. The show didn't end until midnight and the audience was so wrung out that they just sat in their seats for a good ten minutes trying to get up the strength to leave. The band, on the other hand, was pumped up and rarin' to party, especially Billy Ray. I took Candy Jr. backstage figuring I owed it to her to let her be the life of the party and she was...for about ten minutes. The last I saw of her and Billy Ray, she had a bottle of tequila in one hand and, uh..., well. let's just say the other hand was full too. Billy Ray's wife was laying a backbeat on the drummer and appeared to be settling in for a long set. Fatbutt was in the corner counting money while the rest of the band and the back-up singers chose up sides for the orgy.

I already mentioned Toe Jam and Veronica and it looked like everybody else was taken care of so I opted for bed. Sometimes I do learn.

forty two

"Wherein a pleasant surprise manifests itself..."

By Monday morning, the Billy Ray Muckenfuss caravan had moved on to wreak havoc in another location and most of the county had nursed themselves back to some semblance of sanity and sobriety; word was that even Toe Jam had recovered consciousness but was regretting the fact. Even Z.Z. had seemingly recovered from the ravages of Veronica and was preparing himself for Natasha's return to his loving arms.

We were having a morning pick-me-up in Katie's and he was in one of his more philosophical moods.

"Lordy, Bubba, sometimes I think I oughta just go ahead and marry ol' Natasha and get it over with. My health would probably be the better for it but what if...?"

His voice trailed off and I knew that some little sweet thing had probably just come through the front door and interrupted his train of thought, such as it was.

Sure enough, a vision of femininity was walking toward the bar, if walking was the proper term. It was more like some kinda slink crossed with a glide with a little grind thrown in for good measure. I reached for my Manatee malt, Z.Z reached for his comb and the girl reached the bar and ordered a "Screaming Orgasm". I choked on the malt, Z.Z dropped the comb and the girl just smiled and said, "Run me a tab. I'll probably have more than one!"

There was something about her that made her familiar but I couldn't put my finger on it; no pun intended. Her black hair was pulled back into a pony tail that reached her waist and what at first appeared to be a killer tan proved at second glance to be her natural color confirmed by the biggest, blackest almond eyes either of us had ever seen.   Z.Z. recovered first:

"Hi there. My name is Captain Cook and I want to sail to your island and be converted to paganism, hedonism, cannabilism or whatever isms you're willing to share."

"Well, Captain, you look a little skinny for the stew pot so I think I'll pass."

"But we could fit together in a hot tub real fine, I'll bet."

At this she just snickered and had a sip of her drink. Being the couth gentleman that I am, I offered my hand and introduced myself. "My name's Bubba Convoy and this idiot is Z.Z Ryder. We are harmless for the most part but do get a little silly in the company of young ladies of the beautiful persuasion."

"Well, thank you, sir. My name is Jasmine Kahunatuna and I've gotten used to a certain reaction to my genetic good fortune."

It took about two seconds for the last name to register and then it hit me; this was Sam's daughter. The pride and joy of our local sheriff. In that same two seconds, I realized that, for the sake of maintaining our somewhat tenuous relations with Sam, it was in our best interests to show the young lady that we were merely passing some light banter with no harm intended.

Z.Z, however, had yet to recognize the name and, blinded by pulchritude, insisted on another effort at innuendo.

"Honey, I must say that your genes and your jeans make a great combination. Wanna share a little DNA?"

I decided it was time to step in and stop Z.Z before he wound up feeding Ol' Bogey for another ninety days or, worse yet, being fed TO Ol' Bogey if Sam got wind of his hittin' on Jasmine. But I didn't get the chance.

"Now, Clyde, whatever will I say to Daddy and Natasha Sue when you and I are seen romping around the county like a couple of horny armadilloes?"

Well, the Daddy didn't register with Z.Z. but the Clyde and Natasha Sue did.

I choked on the Manatee Malt again as I realized this gal was on to us and had set us up for a real take-down.

"Katie", she hollered down the bar, "Buy these two clowns a drink on Daddy. Lord knows they look like they need one."

Katie sat two malts in front of us grinning like she just won the lottery and shaking her head as if to say, "You boys have met your match now. This one'll keep you on your toes or maybe on your best behavior."

"Okay, you two. Daddy warned me about you guys but said if I set you straight, you'd be friends to rely on and someone to cover my back. Looking at the two of you, I'll just have to take Daddy's word although if I was going to pick a couple of big brothers, I might have shopped around for another day or two."

Z.Z. hadn't closed his mouth yet but I was grinning like an idiot with the realization that here was a real girl, living in the real world and probably just about as much wacko fun as we were. Of course, wearing hot pants or a Wonder Bra could pose a problem when it came to joining our boys' club but I was willing to overlook her shortcomings(?).

The next day, Sheriff Sam caught up with us over at Sidepocket Simpson's and folded himself onto a bench as we finished a game of nine-ball.

"Well, well, I hear you two degenerates met a certain young lady yesterday? And were somewhat smitten until her family connections were revealed."

"Sheriff, her high moral character was evident the minute she walked in and far be it from me or Patrick to make untoward remarks to one of such a fine demeanor."

Well, coming from Z.Z., that startled both me and the sheriff to silence.

Then Sam spoke, "Ryder, that's about as much bull as I can stand but she did say you boys were about what I told her to expect. And, I might add, she's used to a lot worse. Anyhow, she's down here on a grant to study the coral reefs and she'll need some local knowledge from time to time. I know you boys have some expertise." Sam was obviously referring to our experience with the eel.

"Sure, sheriff, we'll be glad to help her any way we can." This said though I was not especially happy with the idea of spending a lot of time with Miss Jasmine as she paraded around in a wet bikini.

Thus it was that Jasmine became "one of the boys", if you can call that package a boy. Somehow, we learned to ignore the curves and bulges in her wetsuit and the expanse of skin or whatever when she stripped out of it. Most surprisingly, Natasha Sue took to her easily and even Candy Jr. grudgingly admitted that Jasmine was easy to get along with. So, we became a group of three, four or five; there might be any combination imaginable depending on who had to be where.

forty three

"Wherein we revisit a tragic occasion..."

It's been a while since I mentioned Sis and Ol' Whathisname but I've been busy. Anyhow, Sis called the other day to remind me that it was the anniversary of our Momma and Daddy's untimely demise. We always put some nice flowers on their place over at Sunny Acres Corpse Condominium---a room with a view.

I guess I never mentioned my parents before 'cause it just kinda slipped my mind, it having been fifteen years since the tragic accident that took them from us.

You see, Momma and Daddy took a walk every afternoon with Nuc Mom, their Vietnemese pot-bellied pig. Well, this one afternoon while they were on their usual stroll, Marvin "Stick" Meeks decided to hang-glide off the water tank on the edge of town. Now Ol' Stick weighed about four-hundred pounds as near as anybody could tell; that's how he got the name "Stick"; everything he ate tended to stick to his ribs. Any how, Ol' Stick managed to wrassle his glider up to the top of the water tank whereupon he jumped. There has always been some disagreement between observers on the ground as to the precise angle of Ol' Stick's flight path but it was generally agreed that he wasn't much in the way of an aeronautical engineer.

In any case, his trajectory was such that he built up a good head of steam and was goin' like a bat outta hell when, quicker than you can say, "Wilbur and Orville wouldn't a done that!", Ol' Stick simultaneously hit Momma, Daddy, Nuc Mon and the ground resulting in a pileup that would of made Evel Knievel proud. Nuc Mom was the only survivor. So, Sis and I lost our only family, Nuc Mom was an orphan and the "all you can eat" buffet down at Alfonso Jazeera's Two Hump Cafeteria and Feed Store began to turn a profit for the first time in years.

So, I met Sis at Sunny Acres and we paid our respects to our dearly departed parents. I took a nice bouquet of flowers that I found in the dumpster back of Elvis "I do!" Gump's Wedding Chapel and Small Appliance Repair Shop. Sis made me remove the "Congratulations" banner in spite of my insistance that the sentiment was appropriate for those who had arrived at the Pearly Gates---the fact that it had been fifteen years notwithstanding.

I would have asked Z.Z. to come along but I knew his feelings about cemeteries and such. "Bubba, the only way I'm going there is feet first on a slab and I ain't gonna be real happy then!" Like he had a choice.

With this solemn duty taken care of, I figured I'd best start getting ready for an upcoming event that promised to be the biggest thing to hit Edsel County since Candy Jr. came back from plastic surgery.

forty four

"Wherein Hollywood returns to Edsel County..."

Roll out the red carpet! Rent a tuxedo and book a limo! The word is out; Manny "The Frog", Dot Com and a bunch more of Hollywood's heavy hitters are coming to Edsel County for the world premiere of Manny's movie "Tortilla Flatulence". Word is that there'll be all sorts of media coverage and international VIPs. The Hollywood buzz already has 'Tortilla...'" in the running for an Oscar or two.

I reckon Dot Com just might be a shoo-in for her role as Sister Georgina, a nun who tries to persuade a young girl of the streets (none other than Melanie the librarian her ownself) to clean up her act. Their shower scene is sure to go down in cinematic history. I only saw bits and pieces when they were filming so I don't know how the movie ends yet but I heard it's a real tear-jerker.

Anyway, Dot Com as a nun surely must have brought out the best of her acting talent. Of course, her other talents were well hidden under a bunch of black fabric most of the time. I guess nuns don't much go in for off-the-shoulder or mini habits.

Z.Z. was negotiating with Colonel Joe Bob Finklestein, owner of the Edsel County Drive-in and Skeet Range, to emcee the festivities until I reminded him that he'd have to wear a tuxedo. We agreed that if Natasha Sue spotted him in a tux, she'd be on him in a heart beat with a justice of the peace in tow. She's not one to miss an opportunity like that. So now he's trying to figure out what he can do to participate without having to dress up.

Me, I've already rented my outfit from Miss Charlotte LeBustier's Costume Rental and Feed Store. Miss Charlotte says it's the "Ringmaster Special" and she gave me a discount as it appears I'll be escorting Dot Com down the red carpet. She wants me to be sure and mention her business while we're yakking with Joan and Melissa.

Candy Jr. received an invite to accompany Manny "The Frog" to the premiere and she's having a hard time with it. Seems that the exposure (and we know what that means in her case) might further her ambitions but having to spend the evening, or worse, with Manny is making her hesitate. I suspect she'll bite the bullet and show up on Manny's arm. If I know Candy Jr., she'll upstage Manny so badly people won't even know he's there.

Natasha Sue and Jasmine have agreed to go together as Z.Z has let on to Natasha Sue that he will be involved in important behind-the-scenes matters. No one knows just yet what this entails but, if history is any indicator, disaster may be in the offing.

The rest of the community is likewise in a tizzy what with everybody trying to get in on the act. Katie has leased one of those big old refrigerator trucks, ordered a half ton of conch from the Bahamas and several hundred cases of Manatee Malt. Her place is, of course, party headquarters before and after the movie.

Sheriff Sam has deputized the entire Safety Patrol squad from Edsel County High School for traffic control and appointed the squad commander, Fritz "Skinhead" Wurst, a tempory captain on the sheriff's force. Sam says that Fritz and his two security dogs, a matching pair of chihuahuas, will keep everybody in line.

So, the tension builds as we all wait for the party to begin. It'll be good to see Miss Dot Com again, if you get my drift. I just hope she's in need of a little relaxation like before. I sure am.

"Douse the lights and roll it!"

forty five

"Wherein stars descend and Edsel County rises to the occasion..."

Whooeee! Talk about your basic orgy! We've had some good times here in Edsel County but you can't beat Hollywood to put a party over the top. If there's one person in the county that's not still nursing a hangover, scratches and bites, terminal hickeys or worse, it's would likely be Miss Fern, the librarian, and I'm not real sure about her. Rumor has it that after the premiere, she was seen over in the back bay cavorting in the moonlight with some old dude that critiques movies for one of those nudie magazines---_Wrinkles & Health_ or some such.

I never woulda guessed old Manny had the pull that he used to get some real top H'wood types down here. Hey, Erik Estrange, Mickey Barfo, Paris, Anna Nicole and a bunch of others of lesser talent and stature were right here mixing it up with the locals. As planned, I spent lots of time with Dot Com and even got to walk the carpet with her. Some said I looked a little peaked that night but they just blamed the TV lighting. Little did they know I had a bad case of the Dot Com flu.

Bless Z.Z.'s black heart, he got a job tending to Anna Nicole's little puppy dog so he could get a chance to see her, "...other two little pink-nosed puppies." Apparently, he tended them for a while too 'cause he's been giggling every time I see him. Natasha Sue hasn't been able to pin anything on him, however, so he's happy about that too.

Melanie showed up with the big oriental action star, Hung Lo or Lee or something like that. She spoke to me briefly and said she was going to be in his next flick, "Godzilla and Mothra Get Married". Can't wait for that one!

Like I said, Katie's was party central for the duration and I don't think she closed the doors for at least 3 days. I know I spent at least one full night there hiding under the bar. Dot could get a little wearing on the nerves and something else after a while.

Yep. It was party, party, party but everybody was pretty straight when the night of the premiere rolled around. It was quite a show! They had those big old rotating spot lights outside the drive-in and it looked like London during an air raid. I think about every crew cab pickup truck in the county had been pressed into service seeing as how there aren't too many limos in these parts. Most of the boys had removed the gun racks in response to Sheriff Sam's request. He said they were bad for the county's image.

The emcee duties were turned over to Merle "Golden Tonsils" Wheeler from our local AM radio station, WEDC. Merle never was the brightest bulb in the chandelier and he was best known for playing the National Anthem and signing off the station at noon on his first day there. His reasoning was that AM meant getting off the air before PM. Merle handled it pretty well for the most part. His only flub came when Anna Nicole came down the carpet in a gown cut down around her knee caps. He meant to say she had a "bit" part in the movie but "bit" came out a little off if you know what I mean. Most folks that caught it agreed it was a good description of her role.

Yeah, the premiere went off without a hitch if you don't count Paris pulling a little "Basic Instinct" action when she climbed out of one of the pickups. One of the TV cameras caught her from a low angle and, in five minutes, the boys in the trailer were getting bids for the film from around the world.

I know you're wondering by now if the whole deal went off like clockwork. You gotta be kidding! You know us well enough by now to know better. Besides you must of read about it in the "National Inquisitor"

forty six

"Wherein the revelry takes a turn
for the worse..."

Like I said, the actual premiere went real smooth other than the aforementioned incidents. The trouble didn't start until about mid-way thru the party at Katie's.

Now you gotta realize that this was a major happening for folks hereabouts and everybody was in a party mood. And, that's probably the understatement of the year.

Everything was going smoothly until about midnight which was about the time that most of the crowd was getting a good buzz on and really getting down to serious partying. Our local band, Semi-hole and the Half Assed Indians was cranked and the crowd was gyrating something fierce.

It was about that time that someone noticed Paris was standing topless behind the fish tank. The idea being that the distortion would put her on a par with Anna Nicole cup-wise. Now you know that Anna Nicole ain't gonna stand still for that monkey business so the next thing you know, she's bare breasted behind the tank and the dancing has come to a standstill. I've seen lesser udders on a Holstein.

While the crowd is whooping and hollering and enjoying the view, Candy Jr. is watching the action and none too happily. You see, she's always had the upper hand around here in the pulchritude department and this show threatened to diminish her assets as it were.

At this point, I'd better explain that the majority of the gentlemen of Edsel County have never had the pleasure of viewing these assets unencumbered---present company excluded. Far be it from me to flaunt my credentials but I can attest that Candy Jr. possesses both quality and quantity. From what I had seen, Anna Nicole had the quantity but was lacking that certain quality that separates the girls from the Girls.

Katie was just about to put a stop to this madness when Candy Jr. stepped in front of the tank, pulled her gown down to her waist and took a deep breath. Time stood still---the moon blushed---the inrush of breath in the room cleaned the dust off the overhead fans. Slowly, Candy Jr. took an ice cube and---well, let's just say that the other gals pled *nolo contendre*. Sheriff Sam moved to restore a little decorum to the party but was a tad late as just about that time, Anna

Nicole picked Paris up and deposited her headfirst into the tank. What ensued is what made the papers.

First, there's Paris in the fish tank with a big orange, black and white koi nestled in her nether regions. Next, Anna Nicole has assumed a karate stance daring anyone to defy her lest they wind up with Paris. Best of all and the one that made the front page of the Inquisitor is Sheriff Sam with his arms around Candy Jr. covering her "assets". His story is that he was trying to pull up her gown but his hands slipped and he wound up groping Miss Cantaloup. Fortunately, Sam is a widower and is now enjoying the celebrity normally accorded a lottery winner. Which, in a way, I suppose he was.

In the meantime, I was enjoying the envious looks from the young men of the county who came to seek Dot Com's autograph. She held court off to one side of the room and insisted I sit close as a guard against some overly amourous film buff. Every now and then, she would plead writer's cramp and insist on flexing her hand, usually on the inside of my thigh. Mind you, I'm not complaining. I figured one more night wouldn't kill me. I never learn.

Well, the excitememt didn't stop there. I guess the sight of Paris, Anna Nicole and Candy Jr. persuaded some lesser endowed ladies to attempt to convince their significant others that they had talents far beyond mammary perfection. That and events to follow meant that the guys would reap rewards far beyond their expectations

How about that? A whole chapter without a mention of Z.Z.! Here's the reason.

forty seven

"Wherein the ultimate surprise is revealed..."

Through all this melee, no one had missed Z.Z. other than Natasha Sue who had resigned herself to being Jasmine's date and wondering just what he was up to.

I had spoken to him only briefly the last couple of days seeing as I was busy with Dot Com and he was likewise taken up with the "puppies".

It was unlike him to be absent from the festivities of the evening and I was beginning to wonder what undertakings had kept him away. On the other hand, I considered it a blessing that he had not contributed to the earlier debacle.

Thus it was that I was being groped by Dot Com, the triad of Paris, Anna Nicole and Candy Jr. had been returned to what might be termed a more modest state and the revels continued as before.

I don't recall the hour but it was approaching overdose when I saw Z.Z come through the front door. At least the head looked like his. The body was covered in a dark two-piece suit under which was a white shirt and conservative striped necktie. His hair was trimmed, his face clean-shaven and---Ohmigod!---he's wearing socks!!!

My first thought was "Who died?"

He walked stiffly over to where Dot Com and I were sitting and said, " Bubba, can you help me out for a minute?"

With some difficulty, I rose from my chair and asked what I could do.

"Let's go over yonder where Natasha Sue and Jasmine are sittin' for a minute."

The girls had been dancing and having a great time with various local guys who kept hoping that one or the other of the girls might give some indication of interest. Not likely.

I followed Z.Z. across the room and as we approached the girls' table, I saw them do a double take at the apparition that upon closer inspection proved to be none other than Clyde "Z.Z." Ryder.

"Evenin', Jasmine. Evenin', Natasha Sue." Z.Z. was about as formal as I had ever seen him. "You ladies look mighty lovely this evenin'. "

By this time, Jasmine is turning to me as if to say, "What the ..." I in turn shrug my shoulders in a "Beats me." gesture.

Natasha Sue is catching flies in open-mouthed wonder when Z.Z speaks. "Honey, I know I'm not the most attentive man in the world but all this goings on has made me realize that I need to settle down and I figger you're the best I'm gonna do so let's do it."

'The best you're gonna do...? Excuse me, Clyde Ryder. Maybe I'm still looking for the best I can do and I don't think you're it!"

"Aw, honey, you know what I mean. I won't find nobody better'n you and I'm not lookin' for anyone else."

Well, after all this time, I figured Natasha Sue would jump on this deal but now she had decided to play the old hard to get game. I was beginning to worry that Z.Z might find this to be a way out and it would be a long time before we passed this way again.

"Natasha Sue Riggsbee, I love you and I want you to be my wife!" With this, Z.Z. reaches in his pocket and pulls out a ring--not just any ring---this thing looked like the Hope diamond compared to what we were used to seeing.

At this, Jasmine's mouth is going like a dying guppy and I'm having a real hard time breathing too.

"Clyde, I...". Now there are three of us that can't breathe and Z.Z. looks like he might faint from sheer terror.

"Clyde, I...".

This goes on for about a minute. Natasha Sue with the, "Clyde, I..."; Z.Z. looking like a new puppy that just chewed up your Manolo Blahniks; Jasmine is looking at the both of them still speechless and I'm sure I'm hallucinating from God knows what.

Now surprise is one thing and practicality is another. A second look at the diamond brought Natasha Sue down to earth and quicker than you could say, "Third finger, left hand.", she had popped that ring on her finger and made it official. Z.Z was spoken for.

It took another minute or two for us to realize what had just taken place. When the spell broke, Jasmine grabbed Natasha Sue in a big hug and I just sorta stared at Z.Z. until he gave me a lopsided sheepish grin and said, "Well, I guess that tears it, don't it?"

My brain was still about two minutes behind what was happening and it wasn't until Jasmine grabbed me by the arm and made me hug Natasha Sue that I came to my senses. Pretty soon, Z.Z., Natasha Sue and I were hugging like long lost kin and then Jasmine jumped into the grope and added a whole new dimension to the word friendship. This was the first time I'd been that close to her and I sure hoped it wouldn't be the last.

It took a few minutes for the news to circulate around the room and the reactions ranged from sheer disbelief to hallelujahs.

No one in Edsel County had ever needed an excuse to party but, given one, they usually do it to excess. This was the case with the engagement. You would have thought a royal wedding was imminent. Guys that had been denied bedroom privileges used the occasion to hint that they too might be on the verge of the big move. The same girls who had been holding out decided that maybe a little incentive was needed to get their suitors motivated. This resulted in an evening of copulating couples unequalled in county history. Aside from the bedside benefits realized by Z.Z., he was the happy recipient of free drinks from a number of satisfied suitors who credited him with unlocking the chastity belts of numerous girl friends.

On the other hand, I knew that in the future, he would get blamed for the ball and chain that many wore. Res ipsa loquitor!

forty eight

"Wherein pending domesticity is sorely tested..."

The fallout from the premiere was actually less than might have been expected. Aside from some monumental hangovers, various aches and pains from bedroom contortions and the usual domestic complaints, there was precious little to bitch about.

The Hollywood crowd, including Melanie and Hung, Manny, Dot Com and the rest returned to the left coast to lobby for the Academy Awards. Candy Jr. had abandoned her Hollywood hopes for the time being and had occasionally been seen accompanying Sheriff Sam on his rounds. It seems that the sheriff's ability to cover an "asset" with one huge hand had piqued her curiosity as to the size of other of his anatomy.

There was still some disbelief over the formal engagement of Z.Z. and Natasha Sue. Skeptics gave it about a week, meaning until about the next week's happy hour at Katie's when Z.Z. made his usual foray searching out the latest innocent young lovelies that happened to wander into the bar in search of weekend excitement. I had to admit that I was among those who seriously doubted his ability to honor this unexpected commitment. Natasha Sue had also expressed some doubts to Jasmine which were relayed to me with the caution that I might somehow be held responsible if our boy strayed from the straight and narrow. This was a responsibility that I had no stomach for.

Fortunately, Katie had appointed herself the guardian of Z.Z.'s fidelity and made it known to one and all that if he started catting around the Conch House, he would, at best, be declared persona non grata and summarily cutoff at the bar. Z.Z. was none too happy with this arrangement but did admit that it probably was for the best. "Bubba, I reckon I need a watchdog during this deal but it ain't gonna be easy. Why just the other day...". I stuck my fingers in my ears and walked away.

As you know, we've had some wild adventures that involved female companionship and it looked like we were approaching the end of that life. Mixed emotions would probably best describe what I felt but, at the same time, I felt that Z.Z. needed to do the right thing by Natasha Sue.

In the meantime, like I said, Melanie had gone off to Hollywood, Candy Jr. seemed to have taken up with Sheriff Sam and I was left with a terminal case of lonesome.

Fortunately, Jasmine's project was under way and we were pretty busy surveying the offshore reefs. At least three or four days a week, weather permitting, we were out on the water snorkeling or gathering samples and taking photographs. The betrothed couple would join us occasionally and Jasmine and I had to bite our tongues to avoid asking about any pending wedding plans. Other than the impromptu engagement, little action had taken place in regard to any impending nuptials.

Jasmine would ask now and then just what I thought the odds were that the wedding would ever happen. I told her that I figured it was 60-40, pick your side either way. While the initial step had been taken, I was only too aware of Z.Z.'s propensity for personal calamity. I'd been there through too many. You see, I do learn.

Sure enough, a couple of weeks later, I'm sitting in Katie's with Jasmine when Z.Z. comes sidling in and motions me to meet him in the men's room. Now, I know this can lead to no good but I excuse myself and answer his summons.

"Bubba, I need a favor!" This is trouble and I know it.

"No, no and no!" is my reply 'cause I know this is going to lead someplace I don't want to go.

"Listen, Bubba, you gotta help. It's not my fault, I swear. I stopped for gas down at Fouad's 24-hour Gas-up and Veterinary Clinic and who pulls up beside me but that redhead from Delray Beach that I met last fall. You remember, the one with the squeaky voice and the squeaky toys?"

Somewhere in the back of my mind I recalled his recounting a tale of debauchery that ended in his escape from

149

her clutches when she headed back north on a Sunday evening.

"I thought you were glad to be rid of that experience?"

"Aw Bubba. That was last year. I need just one more little wild time before I give it up forever. She's down at Holiday Isle with a girlfriend and wants me to join them. Sez the girlfriend is good but they need a little something extra. Wanna go?"

Now, I'm not about to get involved in this scheme. I don't want Natasha Sue to be gunning for the both of us.

"NO! N-O spells no! And if you're smart, you'll forget this and get your skinny butt home. I'm not covering you on this deal!"

"Okay then. I'll just have to come up with another story. An all night fishing trip for swordfish oughta cover it. But, Bubba, we could share the fun."

Yeah, If I shared the pleasure I would probably wind up sharing the pain and most of the blame. Maybe I'm learning.

forty nine

"Wherein intuition proves correct..."

Yeah, the engagement is off and you can guess the reason why. Z.Z. went ahead with his plan to go to Holiday Isle and meet up with the redhead. He just up and took off without a word to Natasha Sue which automatically got her sonar in tracking mode and she was looking for a firing solution. (I learned that from one of those submarine movies on cable.)

Of course, the first thing she did was come looking for me and I could tell she was kinda surprised to find me on my usual stool at Katie's.

"Bubba, have you seen Clyde today? I haven't heard a word from him since yesterday afternoon!"

Now I've got me one of those dilemmas. If I say I don't know, I'm lying outright to a good friend but I sure can't tell the truth at the risk of abetting manslaughter. I figured the next best thing was sorta the truth.

"Well, he mentioned something about going sword fishing tonight with Captain Albury on the Pea Pod. He wanted me to go but I had to spend the afternoon with Jasmine getting ready for tomorrow plus I needed to get a good night's rest."

That's sorta the truth, right? I mean he did mention sword fishing, right?

"Humph! He'd better come back smelling like a mullet that's been in the sun all day! Fishing, my patootie!"

With that, she stomped outta Katie's and I was off the hook, at least for the moment.

Unfortunately for Z.Z., Natasha Sue is a pretty bright lady, especially when it comes to the frailties of her betrothed. By the time she reached her car in Katie's parking lot, she had decided to check the Pea Pod to see if it was in its slip and, if so, where was the most likely place to find the wandering Z.Z.

Needless to say, the boat was tied snugly to the dock with no sign of action thereabout. With her brain now in high gear, Natasha Sue did a fast scan of Z.Z.'s options. There were four. The first three options, fishing, drinking with me at Katie's or being with her had been eliminated. This left the fourth option which meant another woman was involved. Z.Z. is nothing if not a creature of habit.

The next question was where this might be taking place. She ruled out the Malelucca Lounge because of its reputation as Menopause Manor and Z.Z.'s taste for more nubile companionship. The Tiki Bar at Holiday Isle flashed before her eyes like lightning and quicker than you could say, "Incoming! Duck and cover!", she was on the road headed south.

I got most of the rest of the story from Z.Z the next evening though he was having a little trouble being understood through his puffy lips.

It seems that Z.Z. and the redhead were engaged in a little game of tonsil hockey while sitting at the Holiday Isle Tiki Bar. This is not an unusual practice there and hands occasionally stray into loose clothing. Thus it was that when Natasha Sue happened upon the scene, the happy couple was engaged in what might be termed "heavy petting", meaning that a couple of hands were hidden in the vicinity of each other's nether regions.

If you remember, Natasha Sue works for the newspaper meaning she carries a cell phone, PDA and small tape recorder plus the usual feminine accouterments---all these things in a rather substantial leather handbag with a heavy strap. A formidable weapon to be sure. Unfortunately, with his spare hand, Z.Z. happened to be taking a drink from a heavy mug when the bag hit the back of his head. This resulted in both a big lump on the back of his head and cut lip number one.

It took a moment for the paramours to untangle and a second blow was landed before Z.Z. could get out of the way. The redhead meanwhile, once she was free of Z.Z., backed off to steer clear of the attack.

After a few choice words aimed at Z.Z., Natasha Sue told the redhead to amscray or she would be next. The redhead, however, sensing the situation, decided that she too was a wronged woman and proceeded to attack Z.Z. hitting him with a mug which resulted in cut lip number two. Natasha Sue told her that the solo blow was enough to restore her honor and that she, Natasha Sue, would administer any further punishment.

About this time, security showed up and prevented further damage to our boy. When the situation was explained to them, they politely told Z.Z. that he'd worn out his welcome and best hit the road. Natasha Sue said she'd follow him and make sure he got home all right. A dubious statement in light of her current state.

She did follow Z.Z. home and, according to neighbors' reports, there followed a tirade of verbal abuse until he managed to flee into the house locking the door behind him. It was then that Natasha Sue threw a rock through the living room window and followed it with her engagement ring.

So, it appears that the pending nuptials have, at best, been put on hold. If history is any indication, this too shall pass but it will be a while before that loving couple gets it together again.

Meanwhile, I'm getting the cold shoulder from Natasha Sue who, according to Jasmine, is not sure whether or not I was party to the goings on. I'm waiting for her to ask me what I knew and when I knew it.

Z.Z.'s also acting miffed at me and trying to get me to share the blame. He keeps complaining that I should have stopped him from going.

"Bubba, you know how weak I am. It was your duty as my best friend to keep me outta trouble. Boy, if there had been a midnight train to Nassau, I'da been on it!"

I'm just glad that I avoided this particular disaster. Yep, I'm learning.

fifty

<u>**"Wherein remorse brings détente to a volatile situation..."**</u>

The bust-up of Natasha Sue and Z.Z was the subject of much speculation around the county. Most felt that the long-suffering Natasha Sue had probably had enough this time given the fact that she and Z.Z were formally engaged and all. Unfortunately for Z.Z., the majority of folks felt that he had overstepped the bounds this time and he was getting the cold shoulder from friends and acquaintances alike. Even Katie was giving him the business, slamming a Manatee Malt down in front of him and making sure he paid for every one---nothing "on the house" for poor ol' Z.Z.

I say, "Poor ol' Z.Z." but he brought it on himself and it's doggone hard to feel sorry for him. Whoever said paybacks are hell sure knew what he was talking about.

You see, we were sitting in Katie's the other day when who should come waltzing in but Natasha Sue and she's not alone. It seems one of those blow-dried TV reporters from up in Miami was down doing a little local color and Natasha Sue was acting as his guide.

You know the kind I'm talking about---a fugitive from the George Hamilton School of Tanning, twenty-thousand dollars worth of teeth, spends enough on his hair each week to feed a third-world child and is a poster boy for Banana Republic.

And, you can bet his name ain't Wilbur; at least not for public consumption.

Anyhow, they come in and take a table off to one side sorta out of the way. Now Z.Z. is acting like he hasn't seen them but I can see his jaws working and know he's steaming inside. He's sipping his drink, staring straight ahead and I can tell he's fighting the urge to break something.

Meanwhile, TV Guy is flashing his piano key teeth at Natasha Sue and she's giving it right back with her baby blues. This is not good. I start to think about how I'm gonna get Z.Z. outta there without some kind of incident when he drains the last of his drink, calmly places some money on the bar and waves to Katie with a "Good night, Katie, thanks."

"Bubba, I think I'll head back to the ranch and catch a movie. I've about had it for the evening. See ya tomorrow."

And with that he strolled out of the bar without a glance left or right. I was so relieved that I ordered another Manatee Malt to celebrate.

With Z.Z.'s departure, I noticed Natasha Sue straightened up and turned off the charm she'd been laying on TV Guy. I suspected all along that this was for Z.Z.'s benefit and I also suspected that this charade wasn't over. There was no way Natasha Sue would go any further with TV Guy but I wouldn't put it past her to disappear until about daylight in case Z.Z. was checking on her. This was going to be a big time payback.

The next day, it was obvious Z.Z. hadn't had much sleep and just as obvious was his melancholy. I was still trying to muster up some sympathy for him but it was a trial. He wanted to talk about last night but it was just too painful for him. I dropped a few hints that I knew that it had been an act but I wasn't having much effect on his mood.

"Bubba, I have flat screwed the pooch this time and I don't know what I'm gonna do."

"Well, ol' buddy, I figger the best thing to do is walk the straight and narrow for a while and make it obvious. No making conversation with the strays that wander into Katie's and stay in the public eye until you go home at night--- alone."

"Dammit, Bubba, I miss that gal so much I could just die."

"Listen, just do like I tell you. This is gonna take some time but I think she'll come around and everything will be right again. I'll see if Jasmine will talk to her and find out how she's feeling."

Speaking of Jasmine, we had been keeping pretty busy on the reefs. We went diving or snorkeling darn near every other day and we got along real well together. She took pictures of the reef fish, coral formations and counted the scars caused by yahoos that dropped anchor on the coral and ripped it up.

On days that we worked, one or the other would make a lunch and we'd break around noon, eat and then relax for a while before resuming the afternoon's work.

Now, remember Candy Jr. is hanging with Sheriff Sam and Melanie is off to Hollywood so I have been without feminine companionship for some time. You know what I mean!

So there I am, lying in the warm Florida sunshine with a tanned beauty that would have made ol' Paul Gauguin blush. Talk about your trial. Of course, every time I looked over at her lying on her back with her stomach rising and falling as she breathed, I could just imagine---hold on, forget that!

That was just about the time I could feel Sheriff Sam's presence over my shoulder as if to say, "Think twice, boy. If you want to stay a boy!" A powerful dissuader that!

All in all, I'd have to say that we get along pretty well. Jasmine seems happy with our arrangement and I'm doing my best to think of her as a sister but it's getting harder every day. Somebody once said, "Incest is fine as long as you keep it in the family." I don't know about that one.

fifty one

"Wherein our hero reminisces about past indiscretions, failures and successes..."

Seeing that Natasha Sue and Z.Z. were on the outs and Katie's provided too much of a temptation in the form of wandering female tourists, Z.Z. had taken to spending a lot of time at my place just hanging out. We would take a six-pack of Manatee Malt and sit in the back yard under an old gumbo limbo tree and talk about most everything but the current situation.

I knew his mind was never far away from trying to figure out some way to patch things up with Natasha Sue but I just sorta let it ride while we sat and sipped. I was in a sort of doldrums myself and didn't much care to spend the evenings at Katie's so this was fine with me.

Maybe I should mention at this point that part of my problem was the nearly daily contact with Jasmine. I knew better than to put a move on her but it was becoming increasingly difficult. On the other hand, I was having some strange feelings about her that didn't necessarily involve lust. We seemed to get along together like we could read each others thoughts. Now I did have some thoughts that were better left unread by her. I mean, here's a gal that was peeling out of a wet suit once or twice a day and that act alone was enough to stir up the old libido and make me forget about Sheriff Sam, at least for a minute or two.

Anyway, Z.Z. and I would sit and talk about most anything to keep our minds off the women; at least the two women that currently occupied our thoughts.

This is not to say we didn't have some discussions about the fair sex, not to mention the good sex and the better sex. The conversation had started with some high school adventures, mostly unrewarded gropings and grapplings on the beach or in the back seat of various cars which we had managed to restore to some measure of mechanical reliability. Most of these encounters ended in the same way amidst protestations of "...not yet" or "I'm a (insert religion here) and I just can't!" We laughed about one little gal who had been to known to protest on more than one occasion but had finally succumbed to the pleas of a certain back seat Lothario with the feared result.

The girl's father happened to be one of Sheriff Sam's predecessors so the young lady went off to "boarding school" and the Marine Corps gained a recruit who later went on to a distinguished 20-year career, never returning to Edsel County.

I had by this time enjoyed the charms of Candy Jr.'s mother without similar misfortune and we kinda felt, "There but for the grace of God...!"

There was always the usual speculation about which single teachers were getting it on and with who(m). Rumors abounded whenever there was a reasonably young, or not so young, female on the faculty. The poor woman could be as celibate as a nun but stories would surface of her sleeping with everyone from the football team's water boy to the principal, especially if the principal happened to be a woman. There were no bounds to our imaginations. And no shame...

Much greater success had been realized during our brief matriculation at Edsel County Community College and Barber School. Z.Z and I cut a rather wide swath through the ranks of the post-teen debutramps who, if not seeking career training, would settle for a husband who paid most of his bills on time. This was almost my undoing.

Sometime in the midst of this period of debauchery, I met a little gal named Rhonda who, more or less, swept me off my feet. That is, I spent a lot of horizontal time with her. Rhonda had an assortment of talents that outdistanced anything I had experienced thus far in my callow youth. Unfortunately, it never occurred to me to question the origin of such an education seeing as I too enamored of said training.

Thus it was after a particularly grueling weekend, I found that, in the heat of a moment of passionate insanity, I had made some mumbled references to matrimony. References that I was expected to follow up on in short order. When Z.Z. heard the news, he vowed to have me committed under Florida's Baker Act whereupon an individual can be locked up and protected from himself for 72 hours.

He then informed me that the object of my desire had a somewhat checkered past---a revelation he had withheld as it seemed of little consequence until this recent turn of events. It seems Z.Z. and Rhonda had a casual conversation one day in which she had accidentally mentioned a rather infamous private club up in Miami. A discreet inquiry revealed that a certain "Rhonda Ragbag" had been barred for activities that far exceeded the usual depravity of the place.

Z.Z. let her know that if she had any hopes of other marriage possibilities anywhere within a fifty mile radius, I was no longer a candidate. So, I was saved from unholy matrimony by the vigilant Z.Z., a debt I have yet to repay in full.

We recalled affairs short and lengthy, tourists and tarts, real sweethearts and heart breakers. Finally we reached the current era of Melanie and Natasha Sue. Melanie, of course, was no longer in the picture and Natasha Sue was a question mark. At least for the moment.

Finally, our conversations would turn to the subject of Jasmine. The first time this happened, Z.Z. blew Manatee Malt out his nose and had a coughing fit.

"Yeah, Bubba," he giggled when he could breath again. "I can see it now. Sheriff Sam and Candy Jr. and you and Jasmine. Just think, that'd make Candy Jr. your mother-in-law!" This time, I choked on my Manatee Malt.

fifty two

"Wherein there are favorable signs of a thaw..."

It was a given that the stand off between Z.Z. and Natasha Sue would gradually ease 'cause I know she loves the rascal in spite of his shortcomings. It seems Z.Z., bless his heart, composed a letter to Natasha Sue in which he admitted the error of his ways and made some promises that some skeptics would condemn.

Now the mere fact that he sat down and wrote anything got Natasha Sue's attention as he's not known for putting more words together than it takes to sign his name on a Hallmark or bar tab. Had it not been for the highly personal content, I would have begged to read this effort as I was about as surprised as Natasha Sue.

Whatever it was he said in the letter seems to have had the desired effect as they are speaking to each other again. They have even been to Katie's together for dinner and left holding hands. Word is that's about as far as it goes for now; hand holding that is.

So, there seems to be peace in the valley, so to speak, for the time being.

Oh, I almost forgot, the Oscar nominations came out this week and, sure enough, Dot Com made the list for Best Actress. This means I stand a good chance of heading out to Tinsel Town for the ceremony. Dot had promised me the trip if she got nominated. I'm looking forward to seeing all that glitter and glamour and maybe getting a little tune-up while I'm at it.

Right now, I'm more concerned about Z.Z. and Natasha Sue. It's even odds that she'll finally land him but there's no takers either way. I'm trying to stay out of the deal but I love'em both and can't take sides either way.

Meanwhile, I've got enough problems of my own. I mean, Jasmine is not a problem but, yeah, I guess she is. We spend a lot of time together doing her projects and we get along like nothing I've never known. Good Lord almighty, we have more fun working than most folks have when they're horizontal. As they say, "...therein lies the problem"!

Now, Jasmine doesn't have the walking pulchritude of Candy Jr. or the hidden smoldering fire of Melanie, either of which turn a red-blooded American male into a slobbering idiot. I mean, not to sell her short, Jasmine has her own attributes and they surely enough to make me wonder about my intentions. Given other parentage, I would probably have put my best moves on her by now, but the image of Sheriff Sam puts a damper on any thoughts of lust. So, we spend a lot of days together on the water and many evenings with friends at Katie's. These evenings always end the same way; I drop Jasmine off at her apartment, get a hug and peck on the cheek and a, "See ya manana!" Frustation is my middle name.

Meanwhile, Ol' Sanford Mims looks like a shoo-in for the Congress of the US and A. He's been walking the straight and narrow lately while his campaign is in full swing plus his only competition is Lefty Schulman, the one-armed, Jewish alligator wrestler. Lefty's sole platform issue is that he has only one arm to pick your pocket with---he's got a point there.

fifty three

"Wherein serpents enter the garden..."

Here's some breaking news, it seems that a large snake was sighted in the area but the first report came from "J.D." (as in Jack you-know-who) Spiller. J.D. swears his big ol' pit bull, Hortense, got dragged off and swallowed by a snake as big around as a stovepipe. As this supposedly happened around 11 in the morning, the story was suspect as J.D. is usually unable to focus on anything after his breakfast of Tennessee whisky and jelly doughnuts.

Anyway, we had a couple of more reports but most folks were blaming this on the "me too" hysteria like when some nut says he saw a flying saucer. After another dog and a couple of cats disappeared suddenly, Sheriff Sam decided it was time to take action. The missing animals were all from the same general area so he logically concluded some kind of foul play was involved. As he later told the story at Katie's, he found a track in the sand at one of the homes of a missing animal.

"It looked like some drunk had been dragging a sack of flour in the sand except there were no footprints, just this wavy line." Sam continued, "I tracked it for about 30-40 yards but lost it in the marsh back of the house."

He then asked if anyone was willing to maybe drag a big turkey carcass through there to flush the critter out. Of course, he was looking straight at Z.Z. when he said it. Z.Z. allowed as how he didn't even want to see a turkey at Thanksgiving given his last experience with same.

Sam's work gave credence to J.D.'s story and so all the dogs, cats, pigs and little kids went on house arrest till the thing could be sorted out.

It was "Buzz" Dolittle, of all people, who reported the next sighting. He was flying on a mosquito eradication project over the marsh when he saw some kinda strange apparition in the reeds. When he landed, he called the sheriff and gave him directions to the general area. Sam commandeered a mud buggy and off we went..."we" being the sheriff with me and Z.Z. riding shotgun, literally. We had armed ourselves with a pair of 12-gauge pump shotguns from the sheriff's office.

Now, how he does it, I can't figure out but Z.Z. had found a bush hat; you know, the kind with the brim pinned up on one side and he had on a safari vest with enough shotgun shells stuffed in it to sink him if he fell in the water. Only Sam's personal knowledge of Z.Z.'s prowess with the gun kept him from disarming the fool on the spot.

By the time we were geared up to go, Buzz was back in the air and gave us directions by walkie talkie. We hadn't gone more than half a mile when Buzz said we heading right for the spot and what ever it was hadn't moved.

We broke out into a little clearing and---Lord have mercy!--- there was the weirdest thing I ever saw. It was hard to tell whether the snake had tried to eat a gator or vice versa. Each had swallowed about half the other. In any case, both were dead so we got a good look and took some pictures so people would believe us. Sam later called the wildlife troops and they showed up with a snakeologist who identified the snake as some sort of humongous python about 18 feet long.

Seems there's a lot of these critters crawling around South Florida these days what with kids buying them when they're 3 feet long and dumping them when they start drooling over the other family pets. The snakeman said this one was further south than any previously reported and our area really wasn't good habitat for them. Boy! That's a relief; unless they develop a taste for tourists.

fifty four

"Wherein, once again, there's 'peace in the valley', so to speak..."

Seems like there's always some kinda excitement going on around here when it comes to wildlife of various kinds. We've had the chupacabre scare, my adventure with Ol' Bogey and then the snake and gator thing. I figger the next thing will be an attack by walking catfish that I hear are pretty scary or maybe it'll be African bees that are on the march. Whatever, I guess we'll come through none the worse for wear like we always do.

Speakin' of Ol' Bogey, Shank came down from Hilton Head for a little visit and wanted us to play a round with him at the country club. Not withstanding the fact that Z.Z. and I had been banned for life, I wasn't about to go anywhere near that danged thirteenth hole, figgering Ol' Bogey might just have a long memory and, even though our meeting was in the dark, might just recognize me. I hear he's developed a taste for turkey but that doesn't mean he might not want me for dessert.

Z.Z. and Natasha Sue seem to have reached some sort of détante in their love life and my buddy is walking a straight line for the present. He can be a trial but mostly he's entertaining as hell.

Just recently, he was telling me about the new dentist in town, Dr. Hyman "Drill'em and Fill'em" Waldbaum. Z.Z. overheard a conversation in Katie's where a reference to the good doctor included something about bicuspids. Naturally, he twisted this around and his comment was, "Hell, I ain't going to no 'bi-cuspid' dentist like that. All that schoolin' and he can't make up his mind between boys or girls!" I didn't even try to explain.

Lately, I've been having trouble maintaining my regular routine of work with Jasmine and trying to concentrate on whatever it was we were doing. We reached a point where I got a kiss on the cheek every morning when we met and a big hug and kiss on the lips when we finished the day. Did I mention what a trial this was? My libido was taking a beating and so was---never mind!

Anyway, the ever-present specter of Sheriff Sam managed to keep my damper turned down a notch and I remained on my best behavior. DAMMIT!!!

Now that I think of it, it seems Sheriff Sam has been a little busy lately with none other than Candy Jr. They've been seen here and there appearing to be on what might be called "friendly terms". Jasmine has mentioned their relationship once or twice but doesn't seem to be too upset about it. At least Candy Jr. is a few years older than Jasmine. And, she's sorta cleaned up her act, if you know what I mean. The Daisy Mae look has been toned down considerably in deference to the sheriff's high office, I suppose.

I guess I'd better go meet Z.Z and pick out our lottery numbers for tonight. That booger is over 200 million and we don't want to miss out on a big payday. Is this a great country or what?

fifty five

"Wherein prosperity and peace 'of a sorts' come to Edsel County..."

Whoooooooeeeeeeeee, Hot damn and Holy Cow, Batman!!! Guess who hit the lottery? You got it, citizen; yours truly and Z.Z split a dollar ticket and hit that mother for 200-and-some- million George Washingtons, the second biggest pot in history. Our numbers were 2, 8, 14, 27, 36 and 40...that's Jasmine's, Z.Z's, Natasha Sue's and my birthdays in order followed by Candy Jr's hips and bust measurements.

After we bought the ticket at Ben Laden's Jewish Deli and Bazooka Repair Shop, Z.Z. held on to it for safe keeping. The morning after the drawing, he called me in a hesitant, whispering voice, "Bubba, I...you...we...us...", leading me to wonder just what trouble might have befallen us now. He cleared his throat a couple of times and whispered again, "Bubba, I...I...think we done won us the lottery. I've checked and rechecked and I keep matching the numbers. Maybe you better have a look. I'm not seeing too well."

Well, I hightailed it to Z.Z 's and we put our heads together and, sure enough, the state's six and our six came up a match. We kinda stared at each other for a minute and suddenly we're rolling around on the floor whooping and hollering like two possessed holy rollers.

After a minute or two, Z.Z suddenly sat up, punched me and said, "Now what?"

The enormity of what had happened to us was about to sink in and his question was certainly a valid one. What the hell would we do with that much money? Cars, boats, condos, all the Manatee Malt a man could drink in a lifetime?

I told Z.Z the immediate problem was to keep it a secret lest every free loader and hustler south of Orlando would show up looking for a piece of the action.

"Listen," I told Z.Z., "I read that one of those big winners from a couple of years back set up a foundation or trust, you know, one of those tax dodge things. We'd better find us somebody that knows about that stuff before we go grabbing that money or at least what's left after Uncle Sam gets his share."

"Aw, Bubba, can't I get some whip out just to see what it feels like to have a few thousand in my jeans?"

"Better to have those millions in the bank than stuffed in your shorts. Who do we know that can help?"

Well, that stumped us for a while 'cause nobody we knew ever had to worry about having more than about two paydays stashed away. High finance was not a worry in Edsel County. The only lawyer we knew was Toe Jam and his credentials might be considered suspect. However, after considerable debate, we decided that Toe Jam was our only candidate for immediate advice.

"Boys, you've come to the right place. For years I've been hoping for a chance to practice my true calling. My MBA has lain fallow for many years as I found the lawyering a bit more lucrative hereabouts what with the divorce and personal injury statistics in the area. I have, however, kept abreast of the times and am prepared to offer my financial and business acumen in your service."

Well, we figured Toe Jam's advice was better than anything Z.Z. or I could come up with so we retained the estimable Toe Jam Jones as counsel and that was the beginning of RyCon Holdings LLC and the ConRy Foundation.

fifty six

"Wherein a threshold is crossed..."

The excitement of the lottery win would soon spread throughout the county as winners are in the public domain once the prize is claimed. Everybody in the county knew the winning ticket had been bought at Ben Laden's and speculation about who was the winner was the topic of the week. We managed to keep the secret for about two weeks while Toe Jam set about protecting as much of the money as he could from the Infernal Revenue Service.

The hardest part of the deal was keeping Z.Z. under control while we waited for Toe Jam's magic. The idea that he could go up to Miami or Lauderdale and buy the biggest pickup truck in the land was scalding his butt. Plus, he couldn't decide between a Hummer with every option known or one of those Italian sports cars where your butt drags the ground at about 200 MPH.

Another difficult task was not telling the girls right away. We finally decided to confide in Natasha Sue with the promise that she would get an exclusive interview that would make the national news when we claimed the prize and she could go with us to Tallahassee for the event.

Keeping it from Jasmine was another story. We talked often about her work and the need for more research into saving the important national resource that was the keys' coral reef. The government had made a stab at it by naming the keys a protected area but there was so much more that could be done.

One day during a pause for lunch, Jasmine started on a familiar theme, "Bubba, I've spent days and weeks applying for grants to upgrade my work and establish a center for keys research using interns from the various state marine programs but not much is happening. I can afford my work but not much else."

At that instant, I decided to make a move that would either make or break my life. I had to do it before she knew about the money so I could be sure that her feelings were honest and she could feel that I wasn't trying to buy into her life.

"What's for dinner tonight? I asked innocently. "Lets cook something and enjoy a quiet evening together. I don't feel like Katie's tonight"

"Sure, why don't I stop by the market and pick up a snapper and some veggies?"

"Sounds fine, I'll bring the wine."

Seven o'clock found me driving to Jasmine's as jumpy as that ol' boy, Don Knotts, that used to be on television. I didn't know exactly what I was gonna do but something had to be done and tonight was the night.

Well, all I can say is, it was an evening to remember. We had a glass of wine while she puttered around the kitchen and before I knew it, I had walked up behind her and put my arms around her; being careful not to touch anything serious, you understand; and mumbled something about how great this was.

She spun around and I thought I was in for it but she pushed up against me and before you could say, "Lucy, you got some 'splain' to do!", Jasmine said, "It's about time!" and gave me a kiss that made me forget Candy Jr., Melanie, Dot Com and all the other girls I'd ever enjoyed liplocking with. When we broke apart, which seemed like about 5 minutes later, I couldn't breathe or talk. So I did what any red blooded All-American boy would do, I went back for another. Second verse; better than the first!

"Patrick..." Uh oh, here it comes! I'm in deep doo doo now!

"Patrick, I think we'd better cook now or we might not get around to it tonight."

"G..., Go..., Good idea." I managed to say which was about the only coherent words I could put together. I backed off and gulped about half the glass of wine while Jasmine just stared at me with a little grin and said, "In the immortal words of one Clyde Ryder, 'Well, I guess that tears it, don't it?'"

fifty seven

"Wherein reality far outdoes fantasy..."

Somehow, I never got around to mentioning the lottery that night, there was just too much other stuff going on, most of which involved lots of kissing and groping---up to a point. I wasn't about to screw up this deal by letting lust overcome common sense. (How's that for the new Bubba?) We mostly just went over the time we had been together and how well it went both working and socially.

Jasmine knew about Z.Z. and me and our wild oats, so to speak, but she said right up front that she had seen what she thought was my better side and was quite impressed. It seems even Sheriff Sam had put in a good word for me by saying that he knew I had potential if someone could just harness me. I almost fell off the couch at that bit of news but allowed as how it might be true if the right rider tried to break me.

"Well, I just might climb up on that hoss and see if I can hang on!", she giggled.

The evening went on that way with us just sorta kidding around between clutches. We knew we were close to crossing the line but it just didn't seem to be the exact moment. Anyhow, 'long about midnight, the yawns were starting to interrupt the kisses so we decided to call it a night. That was when I came up with a little plan.

"What's up for tomorrow?", I asked. "Do we have anything hot going on?"

"Nothing in particular. Why do you ask?"

"I have some business to take care of in the morning and I want you to go with me to Toe Jam's office."

"Toe Jam's?" With a little squint. "What's the problem?"

"No problem, just a little business that you might find interesting."

"Okay. I'll meet you there. What time?"

"Make it about eleven and we'll go somewhere for lunch after."

"Will do. Think we can do one more kiss before you go?"

And so we did and then did some more and suddenly the waves crashed on the beach and the train entered the tunnel. Sheriff Sam never entered my mind.

fifty eight

"Wherein we visit the 'nouveau riche'..."

It turns out that Toe Jam had been doing his homework all along and was up to date on all the latest tax dodges laws and was a flat expert on how to save us money and, in fact, where to put it to make some more. I never understood ten percent of what he said about all this and all Z.Z wanted to know was when he was gonna get some "whip out" cash.

When Jasmine and I went to his office, he wasn't too sure about what was up because he assumed I still hadn't told her about the lottery. We passed a few minutes in idle chatter with Jasmine looking a little perplexed about the whole thing.

About then, I turned to her and asked, "Just how much money will it take to do this Marine Institute thing you've been talking about?"

She looked at me real strange and thought for a moment and said, "I've applied for maybe two hundred and fifty thousand dollars over the past six months. If most of that came through, I could run a pretty good program for a couple of years."

"Toe Jam, you think you could scare up about twice that to help Jasmine here out on this deal?"

Toe Jam cleared his throat in his most business-like fashion and replied, "Patrick, I see no problem with that, in fact, we need something of that sort to ameliorate some of the tax debt. Jasmine, how do you want it doled out?"

At this point, Jasmine's eyes are going back and forth between Toe Jam and me just like at a tennis match.

Toe Jam again: "We'll need to set up a non-profit structure to receive the money but I'll get on that right away. Do we have a name for such a thing?"

"Don't worry about that right now." I said, "We'll talk it over and get back to you."

"Wha...what are you two talking about? What in the world's going on?"

"Jasmine, it seems that Msrs. Convoy and Ryder have somehow managed to win the second biggest jackpot in Florida history and are the unworthy recipients of hundreds of millions of Uncle Sam's dollars. My job is to see that it's well-spent and your project certainly fits the bill."

"You're telling me that Patrick and Clyde are now worth millions?"

"Yes, my dear, that's exactly what's come about and you are to share in their good fortune."

I guess I expected her to leap into my arms at that moment but she just stared at me with a funny look. Not a good sign.

"Patrick, we have to talk. Right now!" And with that she stood up, took my hand and walked me outside.

I guess you can see what's coming. Jasmine's first thought was I had planned all this beginning with last night and this was a sort of payback or pay up front, if you will. It took several days and a lot of convincing by Natasha Sue and Z.Z. that this was aboveboard and my intentions were honorable. Natasha Sue told her that this was as much Z.Z.'s idea as mine which helped somewhat. Surprisingly, it took Sheriff Sam to finally make his daughter believe I was serious about the whole deal and her as well.

Oh yeah, I went to the sheriff and had a long conversation about the situation. It took some doing but he finally believed me when I said this was a once in a lifetime deal and I intended to see it through. I did the "L word" and the "M word" for good measure.

As I left his office, he mumbled something about "...Bubba Convoy, my son-in-law! Jeeezus!"

fifty nine

"Wherein plans are revealed..."

Just like we figured, every preacher within a hundred miles swooped down on Edsel County looking to convert us to whatever "ism" they were working at the time. That and the assorted mooches and muggers forced us to flee the county and take up residence at the Ritz Overbuilt Resort in Marco Island. At least we had a suite with all the modern amenities such as a hot tub and large refrigerator full of Manatee Malt. Marco was a pretty good place to hide out as we were close to Goodland and Everglades City, both places that were a little bit more like home.

Toe Jam had rented us a car in his name and we had checked in at the Ritz as the Kamarazov brothers; Ken and Kevin. Nobody looked at us funny when we checked in and I guess at a thousand bucks a night we could have called ourselves the Bobbsey Twins and nobody would have noticed. Anyway, we changed our wardrobes a bit to blend in with the other tourists on the island. Sandals with socks, plaid shorts and Hawaiian-looking shirts and straw hats were our sacrifice to anonymity. Z.Z. allowed as how he wasn't about to go to Everglades City for some fresh stone crabs looking like, "...some kinda fugitive from Fire Island!" I had to agree with him there so we stashed some flip flops, ragged tee shirts and old ball caps in the car so we could change on the way.

Before we left home we bought a private fax line and cell phone for Toe Jam and cell phones for me and Z.Z., Natasha Sue, Jasmine and Sheriff Sam. These were for our use only and nobody else was to know the numbers. We had a fax in our suite so we could send stuff back and forth with Toe Jam. It seems we had a lot of signing to do.

Toe Jam was now working for us full time and he was busy shuffling the money around to avoid giving most of it to Uncle Sam. The ConRy Foundation was the umbrella outfit and in short order was the parent for several non-profits and such. The first one was the Edsel County Sealife Institute which would be the home of the Hawk Channel School of Marine Biology. The school was Jasmine's baby and was our first priority. Various other grants were in the works and as soon as Toe Jam could get everything sorted out, we could go home and try to act normal although we knew that would be a trial.

As it turned out, the tax shelters and some shrewd investments by Toe jam resulted in almost as much money coming in as was going out.

It was almost a month before we returned home and tried to get some kinda normal life going again. Normal life for us included, of course, a big party at Katie's to celebrate our good luck and announce several of the projects which were underway for the county. A free clinic for the fishermen, crabbers and the like and their families was our biggest charity setup and Dr. "Knobby Knuckles" Nolan had agreed to sign on as the head man. We were setting up a grant program for a bunch of things like college tuition for local kids that needed help and cultural improvements; something we knew the area needed.

The party was also the occasion for a couple of other serious announcements---namely the formal engagement of Z.Z. and Natasha Sue (again!) and Jasmine and your truly. Yeah, we did it, big diamonds and all. We had tried to get Sheriff Sam to consider joining us with Candy Jr. but he allowed as how they were happy with the status quo and would pass for now.

For all of Z.Z's talk, he became right frugal when it came to spending money and his only indulgences were the ring for Natasha Sue and a Cadillac pickup truck with all the bells and whistles. We consulted with the girls as to what kind of boat we should get but after kicking it around for several days, it was decided we were all too busy to spend any time cruising around so we put that aside for the foreseeable future.

What spare time the girls did have was spent in planning their dream homes what with marriage now looking like a sure thing and none of the four of us had suitable digs for two people. Z.Z. and I agreed to let the girls have their way as long as the houses included room for a pool table, the biggest flat screen TV money could buy, one of those outdoor kitchens on the patio with a grill big enough for a pig and a bathtub that two people could be comfortable in. The girls and I outvoted Z.Z. on his helicopter pad idea.

So, domesticity seemed to be in the offing and I wondered if, at last, we had finally learned.

sixty

"Wherein an invasion (of sorts) takes place..."

Given all that was happening in our lives at this point, we didn't have much time for playing around and other than a visit to Katie's once in a while, we stuck to business. Even Z.Z. was on his best behavior though he would gaze longingly at the occasional young lovelies that stopped in Katie's for a cool one. It took all the will power he could muster not to offer to buy them a drink as he knew that was the path to perdition.

Still, my ol' buddy was not above a bit of frivolity now and then. Not long ago, I'd been lying on the couch watching a couple of cooking shows; you know the ones with the blond and brunette with the good racks and I don't mean oven racks. Anyhow, those two hotties make up for the little gal that looks like the love child of Tatu, the dwarf on "Fantasy Island". Her name's Yummoh or something like that. Whatever!

So, I'm enjoying the scenery when the phone rings. It's Z.Z. and he's all out of breath trying to tell me something.

"Bubba, (gasp...gasp...) you gotta get down here and see this!"

It takes me a minute or so to find out just exactly where "...down here!") is and what's going on.

It seems Z.Z. was headed to Tommy Turnbuckle's Hardware and Skating Rink when he drove past the old playground and picnic area about half a mile south of Katie's. He spotted some weird goings on and decided to take another look. It apparently looked to him like some strange gathering of egg-shaped deals on wheels.

"Bubba, I figured some mother ship from outer space had spit out a bunch of little eggs and if those things started to hatch, we'd be in a world of hurt. There must be forty or fifty of 'em! I've already put out a call for Sheriff Sam."

Well, knowing Z.Z. as I do, I was sure there was a logical explanation and my curiosity demanded I saddle up and mosey on down there.

Sure enough, what I saw was an approximation of what Z.Z. had described. Scattered around the area were these egg or dome-shaped deals maybe three feet tall with little landing gear wheels on the bottom. They were mostly green and light wisps of smoke seem to come out of most of them.

"Bubba, you reckon those things are Martian eggs getting ready to hatch?"

About that time, we heard a cheer from the other side of the park where a row of campers was parked and then a stream of what looked like relativity normal humans fanned out among the eggs.

"Oh Lord, Bubba! They've already hatched and they look just like us!"

It was about time I sought that logical explanation before Z.Z. went bonkers and did something stupid. Fortunately, one of the humanoid forms spoke up and introduced himself as Floyd from somewhere in Georgia.

"You boys here for the Big Green Egg Fest?"

After we explained our curiosity about the contraptions, Floyd described how these things were highly sophisticated charcoal cookers and owners got together all over the country several times a year and cooked up their specialties.

About that time, Sheriff Sam drove up and when he saw what was going on, broke out laughing so hard he had trouble breathing.

"I had a pretty good idea it was something like this. The first time I saw one of these things it took me a few minutes to figure it out."

Soon, a bunch of the others joined in and explained what was happening. They invited us to join them so quicker than you could say, "Orson Wells ain't got nothing on Z.Z.", we beat feet down to Katie's and grabbed a couple of cold cases of Manatee Malt as our contribution to the festivities.

Well, by the time we got back, the cooking was in full swing and the aromas alone would make your gut growl. These folks knew how to cook.

Us folks in Edsel County could do a mean job with a grill and most anything that needed cooking but these egg crazies did things I'd never seen the likes of. Now most of the food was more or less of the conventional kind, meaning no really exotic meats or stuff. There was one fool that was barbecuing a hunk of boloney on one of those contraptions that must have cost a few hundred bucks. Hell's bell's, everybody knows the only way to cook boloney is to fry a slice in a skillet. Been there, done that!

Anyway, we swapped our Manatee Malt for all kinds of good food and Sheriff Sam told the eggers they were welcome back anytime. Z.Z. and I seconded that motion and we left the "Martians" to party on.

sixty one

"Wherein the gears of matrimony begin to mesh..."

It appears that life as Z.Z. and I know it is coming to an end. The other day, the girls dragged us down to the county courthouse where we picked up the marriage licenses---that being about the most serious thing either Z.Z. or me could remember us doing. I actually thought Z.Z was gonna cut and run about the time it came for him to sign. He was shaking and stuttering something fierce until Natasha Sue whispered in his ear and calmed him down a bit. I could only imagine what she promised him for later but it worked.

I wasn't in much better shape but I got through it and so it was that folks around the county accepted the inevitable although there were a few skeptics who had money riding on the both of us to head for Mexico or further south. At one point, the odds were as much as 3 to 1 on us hightailin' it.

The girls had gotten together and decided the ceremony would be held at the Holy Name of Oral Tabernacle and Used Auto Parts Center out on the main highway. This was about the only place big enough to hold the anticipated crowds that wanted to see this semi-miracle take place. The only other place was the Edsel County Drive-in and Skeet Range but the owner, "Flix" Fontenot, wanted to charge admission and we couldn't go for that.

The reception would, of course, be held at Katie's and she was laying on a couple of tents to handle the overflow. Shuttle buses would run between Katie's and the airport where there would be free parking. I was all for bagging the whole works and taking the girls to Bermuda or someplace like that and very quietly getting hitched but Z.Z. said we couldn't disappoint our friends and neighbors like that.

"Bubba, this will be the biggest event some of these folks have ever seen or heard of outside of the time Bessie Robbins and Joe Tom Hassler got tangled up in the back seat of his VW and the fire department had to cut them out, and with both of them buck nekkid. Now that was a sight to behold. I know Bessie had to go at least 300 pounds and Joe Tom is damn near seven feet tall. I never could figure how they got in the back to start with."

So, things were falling into place and I was accepting the inevitability of what was to come.

By now, surely you've learned that nothing ever goes smoothly in Edsel County. Just when you think all is well, something comes along to disrupt the calm. And come along it did...

sixty two

"Wherein extortion raises its ugly head..."

Whoever said, "Money is the root of all evil." sure knew what he was talking about. It seemed like everybody wanted a piece of our good luck but we went about our business as best we could and let Toe Jam handle most of it. That is until a young lady showed up with a baby claiming it was Z.Z.'s.

Yep! One day this ol' gal shows up at his door and shoves a baby in his face and says it's his son. Now just because he didn't recognize her right off didn't mean the possibility wasn't there. Knowing him as I do, I could believe that his memory might be a little fuzzy when it comes to each and every one of his paramours.

Anyhow, the lady in question had already stopped by Katie's to inquire as to Z.Z.'s whereabouts and, as luck would have it, had mentioned the purpose of her visit.

Now Edsel County's jungle telegraph is about as efficient as they come and most of the county had the word by the time she found him. Of course, Natasha Sue was among the first to know and Jasmine was a close second. This meant that I was soon to under go some serious questioning by both. Claiming ignorance on all counts did little good and I knew we were in for some tempestuous times. As I was to learn later on that day, Z.Z. had denied any and all culpability and the mother went looking for a lawyer.

As soon as we could get together, Z.Z. told me about the encounter and denied any knowledge of the girl. I stood toe to toe with him and made him swear on our lifelong friendship that he was telling the truth. He did and I believed him.

It seems that a shakedown was in progress as the purpose of the visit was to demand that Z.Z. pay an exorbitant sum for child support. This made sense to me and we decided to wait and see what developed.

Of course, in the meantime, here come the girls descending on us with Natasha Sue in hysterical tears and Jasmine trying to comfort her between clenched teeth. It took a while to get the two of them calmed down enough to hold a rational conversation in which Z.Z. once again repeated his innocence and I vouched for his honesty. That didn't do too much in the way of reconciliation but it was a start.

Finally, Jasmine made a suggestion that we hadn't thought of up to that point.

"Z.Z., you can just get a DNA test and that will be that. If you're telling...".

Well, that made sense and Lord knows we needed some at that point. Unfortunately, Natasha Sue was still skeptical and you could have chilled a Manatee Malt with her attitude.

I suggested we just wait and see what the next development would be---mainly to see if she carried out the threat about the lawyer. In the meantime, we gave Toe Jam a heads up and he agreed with our semi-plan.

Within forty-eight hours, Z.Z. had been slapped with a paternity suit demanding he own up to the child and pay five-thousand-dollars a month in support. Apparently, neither this girl nor her shyster lawyer had heard of DNA but that would have to be our ace in the hole. Jasmine's, "If you're telling..." echoed in my ears.

You can bet things were chilly between Z.Z. and Natasha Sue and stayed that way for a few days as she took a "wait and see" attitude. Jasmine wanted to believe but couldn't quite wrap her mind around Z.Z.'s proclaimed innocence.

Dr. "Knobby Knuckles" Nolan arranged for a DNA test for Z.Z. and then the problem became obtaining a sample from the child. The mother declined to cooperate on the advice of her lawyer, one Shelly Sakoshitz, ESQ., AKA the Putz of Paternity.

Consequently, the suit was dismissed on a motion by Toe Jam and we all breathed easier. Actually, some good came of all this as Sakoshitz ESQ turned out to be the father and the girl sued him for support. He was called before the bar association's ethics committee and reprimanded in lieu of disbarment as he needed to work to support the kid.

So, another possible detour on the road to matrimony was avoided and peace descended upon the betrothed. Who knows? We might get this marriage thing done after all.

sixty three

"Wherein plans advance amidst hesitation..."

After the dust settled from this latest crisis and Z.Z. was back in Natasha Sue's good graces, things went along smoothly considering. Our friends and near-friends had gotten used to the idea of us winning all that loot and everybody was happy with the way we had gone about spending it. Toe Jam had done himself proud in setting up the non-profits and such and foundation trustees had been chosen and a few of Edsel County's finest had been named to serve. Chief among these was Sheriff Sam, Sanford Mims and Katie.

Off the wall requests for money didn't let up but Toe Jam and his office staff kept them at bay. The funniest part of the whole business was the offers we kept getting from places like Nigeria and other African nations offering to split enormous sums of money with us if we'd just send them the bank info. We mostly told'em to just hang on to the money for now and we'd get it after it had earned a few more millions in interest.

One major problem that had to be addressed was "THE WEDDINGS". I have to say the girls were pretty cool about the whole deal but every now and then little questions would come up in conversations like, "Why don't we just run off to Tahiti and do it?" Yeah, halfway around the world---the citizens of Edsel County would never forgive us for denying them the closest thing to a royal wedding they'd ever see.

Thus it was decided to have the ceremony where every citizen of the county that wanted to attend could be there. The only venue that could handle the possible crowd was the Edsel County High School stadium and swamp buggy race track so a church wedding at the Holy Name of Oral Tabernacle was out. This was no problem as football season was months away and we were in the dry season so the mud was at a minimum.

Invitations were sent out to all the various rascals that had passed through the county in our recent history such as that Hollywood crowd and Billy Ray and Fatbutt with their entourage.

Of course, there had to be a setback and it came in the form of Z.Z. who, as you might guess, began to have some second thoughts about the whole deal.

"Bubba, I'm not to sure about this getting hitched. Man, this is the end of life as I know it."

"Uh huh, and if you back out now, it'll be the end of your life for sure. If Natasha Sue don't kill you, I will."

"But---but--I'm just wonderin' what happens next?"

"What happens next is you're living with one of the best gals that ever came from around here. And, I might add, doing it legally for once. We have had more luck than any ragass guys like us could reasonably expect and it's time for us to appreciate it."

"Okay, I guess you're right. But it sure is a trial to stay outta Katie's what with all the divorcees and such that have discovered Edsel County as the place to play. Just the other night...".

I stuck my fingers in my ears and said, "Stop it! I don't want to know, so shut up!".

sixty four

"Wherein the nuptials are finalized and miracles are believed in..."

Yes, my friends, it happened. The county's gamblers lost a pile on the final result as the odds were 3 to 1 that it wouldn't happen. But happen it did and without any interference from old girlfriends, boyfriends, relatives and others.

Like I suspected, most of the county turned out to witness what could have been the biggest debacle in memory. There wasn't much debate over my intentions but getting Z.Z. to the altar was an entirely different matter. Admittedly, I was nervous and trying to figure out how to make sure Z.Z. would show up on time. The only thing I could do was to not let him out of my sight from the morning of the ceremony until it was over. I did gain a bit of confidence in him when he asked to borrow a pair of socks.

Thus, at noon, two local gentleman dressed as penguins decided to stop at Katie's for a bit of liquid courage. I must say we cut a dashing figure at the bar as it's not the usual Edsel County dress at high noon on a Saturday.

Not one to let the opportunity pass, Z.Z. was quick to pounce on a couple of tourists of the "...Blonde, I'm here for a good time!" persuasion and I knew it was time to rope him in and head for the ceremony.

So, screaming and kicking, figuratively, I managed to get him out of Kate's and on the way to the ceremony.

Now, you have to realize that most of Edsel County was in attendance and this is not what you might call a sedate crowd. In fact, this bunch could put a South American soccer crowd to shame.

They cheered the preacher, the Reverend Fred from the Holy Name of Oral Church and Repository of Saint Ben Franklins. They cheered all the county politicians except for Commissioner Newt (The Ninny) Newkirk who, it had just come to light, had hired two ex-strippers for office staff at salaries normally granted tenured employees. This in itself normally wouldn't raise the hackles of the local citizenry but Newt had fired the Widow Gaston in order to create the vacancies. The widow, who had been on the county payroll as long as anyone could remember, was a revered member of the community and a repository of Edsel County history.

Anyway, the crowd responded to the commissioner's arrival with a great outpouring of boos, raspberries and not a few one-finger salutes.

(I should point out that RyCon Holdings LLC founded the Edsel County Historical Society and installed the Widow Gaston as president. A wing was added to the county library and named for her.)

As usual, I get sidetracked and go off on another subject.

So, yours truly and the reluctant Z.Z. arrived at the festivities to a raucous welcome of rebel yells and one skeptic in the crowd who kept yelling, "It ain't too late to run!"

It took the arrival of the two brides to quiet them down and the only sound was the sharp intake of breath at the sight of the two most beautiful women they had ever seen.

I whispered to Z.Z., "Now aren't you glad you came?" He just gulped and looked ready to faint. I had already told the preacher to hustle things along as I wasn't absolutely sure that my buddy would make it through a drawn out procedure. And, I also told him to skip the part about somebody objecting to the marriage as it wasn't beyond Z.Z. to plant someone in the crowd to rise up and object at the proper time. I was taking no chances.

Well, the ceremony went like clockwork and before you could say, "Will you...", "I do..." and "I now declare...", it was a done deal. The only thing left was the reception at Katie's which promised to be a humdinger. Let me tell you about it...

sixty five

"Wherein a few final words are written in the saga..."

The reception was held in the parking lot of Katie's under a tent which covered the lot and the surrounding greenery. Billy Ray and his band provided the music and sideshow. That bunch is a hoot sober which is seldom and they outdid themselves (overdosed) on the free booze. They were not alone.

Fortunately, the brides had changed into more appropriate party clothing and it was a good thing as every male over the age of twelve insisted on dancing with one or the other. Z.Z. and I also did our fair share of dancing though it seemed most of our partners were of the blue hair set including Miss Fern Maynard who apparently had a snoot full and insisted on calling me Bubba, a first ever. One lovely who shall remain nameless asked me why I didn't ever marry her. I told her it was because she wouldn't sleep with me. She said, "I will now!"

The food for this melee was provided by Ptomaine Tucker's Catering and Septic Tank Service assisted by Katie, the Major and Chief Figuroa. Jasmine and Natasha Sue had warned them that if the party ran out of barbecue, boiled shrimp and stone crabs, there'd be hell to pay. The aggregate weight of the local folks probably increased by several tons as a result.

The movie crowd was in attendance and drew quite a bit of attention, especially Melanie and Dot Com who signed autographs for the young bucks---mostly on various parts of the boys' anatomy. Manny "The Frog" brought two camera men and a sound guy to film both the wedding and reception an asked for some honeymoon footage but we drew the line there.

Toe Jam and Veronica relit their passion and promised to continue their bi-coastal affair. The wedding once again aroused the mating instinct in many of the county's maidens and they could be seen flaunting their assets at whatever eligible bachelors could be found.

By this time, Z.Z. had accepted his fate and was enjoying himself in spite of earlier misgivings. The two of us hung together throughout the party as we had done for years and we accepted the congratulations of many an envious friend.

At one point during a lull, Z.Z. quietly asked me "Bubba, do you think things will be different now?"

'What do you mean?"

"You know...now that we married'em, do they change? I mean will it be different tonight?

I realized the gist of what he was getting at and replied, "Don't worry, ol' buddy. Everything's gonna be fine."

Finally, the girls said it was time to go so we each a made brief speech to thank everyone and Z.Z added the finishing touch with, "The little women say we gotta go now." I knew he would pay later for "...little women...".

And with that, peace and quiet settled over Edsel County and my ol' buddy and I walked with our brides into the future.

I guess we've learned...

The Players

Patrick "Bubba" Convoy, is co-founder of the ConRy Foundation and RyCon Holdings LLC as well as president and CEO of the Edsel County Sealife Institute, a leader in marine biological and environmental research. He is also a member of the Governor's Advisory Council for Keys Restoration.

Dr. Jasmine Convoy née **Kahunatuna** earned her PhD and now serves as dean of the Hawk Channel School of Marine Biology, an adjunct of the Sealife Institute. She is also the mother of twin boys, Skip and Jack.

The Honorable **Clyde "Z.Z." Ryder,** co-founder of the ConRy Foundation and RyCon Holdings LLC, served two terms as Edsel County Commissioner then subsequently served in the Florida legislature and is rumored to be in line for the congressional seat recently vacated by **Congressman Sanford Mims**. Congressman Mims, former chairman of the House Banking committee, retired to the Cayman Islands for "health" reasons.

Natasha Sue Ryder née **Rigsbee** is the stay-at-home mother of daughter, Rita Rae. When not otherwise engaged in soccer, bake sales, ballet lessons, equestrian lessons and Junior League, she finds time to write self-help books. Her latest, *He Chased Me 'Til I Caught Him,* reached #4 on the New York Times non-fiction list.

Candy Crawford Jr. is head of staff at the Rockin' Double R Ranch, a temporary home for unwed mothers supported by a grant from the RyCon Foundation. She is the common law wife of the local sheriff.

Sheriff Sam Kahunatuna served two terms as the president of the Florida Sheriff's Association and now sits on the Governor's Council of 100. He and his longtime companion, Candace, have four children. The eldest, daughter Florita, is Florida's reigning Junior Miss and a Candy-Striper at the RyCon Clinic.

Katie and the Sergeant Major sold the Conch House and retired to Biloxi where they spend their days at the quarter slots. The Conch House is now The Café Ba-Car-Di where the waiters are all political refugees from Cuban democracy.

T.J. "Toejam" Jones is CFO of the ConRy Foundation. He is a member of the board of numerous financial and charitable organizations. His wife has been confined in a mental institution for the past several years.

Melanie Fenwick is still in Hollywood where she lives with her fifth husband, Richard "The Dick" Wyzewski. They and **Dorothy Comings** are co-owners of Philthy Phlicks Studios and operate a health spa in the San Fernando Valley.

Billy Ray Muckenfuss, after being elected to the Country Music Hall of Fame, retired to Arizona and is the shuffleboard champion of Gila Bend Lakes. His band members elected to remain in Nashville as studio musicians for **Fatbutt Falwell**. **Veronica Velcro** is director of A&R there.

Juan Carlos Bono returned to Peru believing the king gig to be a worthwhile pursuit. He was struck fatally by lightning while attempting to announce his return during a news conference on the steps of a temple in Machu Picchu.

Buzz Dolittle is the corporate pilot for RyCon Holdings LLC's Gulfstream V. This hiring was at the insistence of RyCon's Clyde Ryder who holds great admiration for Capt. Dolittle's safety record.

Dr. K.K. "Knobby Knuckles" Nolan is Chief of Staff at the ConRy Keys Medical Clinic. The clinic provides free out patient medical care for local fishermen, crabbers and their families.

Gilles DeTrop is a lay minister at the Edsel County prison farm. He intends to enter a monastery in Utah upon his release next year.

Miss Fern Maynard applied for a study grant from the RyCon Foundation to be used for research of European library systems. At last report, she was consulting with a young Greek associate on the island of Ibiza.

Shank Bunker qualified for and won the U.S. Open finishing two strokes ahead of Percy Smyth-Churchill. After missing the cut at all four majors the following year, he returned to Sand Spur Dunes as head pro. He shares a condo in Hilton Head with his two pro shop assistants, **Astrud** and **Gunilla**.

Manny "The Frog" Fogelman won a Golden Globe and Oscar for "Tortilla Flatulence" and barely missed the Palm D'Or at Cannes. His next epic, however, "The Wind That Blows Behind" was a flop and Manny was reduced to working for Philthy Phlicks Studios.

Dorothy Comings aka **Dot Com** did not win the Oscar for best actress. Ellen Foster was a heavy favorite and won for her role in "Carpet Munchers On Sunset". Dorothy was gracious in defeat saying, "Ellen had so much experience that it was a natural for her!"

Chief Pepe "Flaming" Figuroa bought a mangrove island out in the backbay, named it Fire Island South (FISO) and it has become THE winter vacation destination for the nation's top interior designers, antique dealers and lady golfers. Pepe also runs the boat service to the island which is known as the "FFF Line"---FISO's Fairy Ferry.

Ol' Bogey is still in the pond on the 13th hole at the Edsel County Country Club. The head golf pro there has added a fifty-cent surcharge to all green fees to provide funds for keeping the old croc in turkeys. It seems he's developed a real taste for turkey and small dogs no longer interest him.

About the author

Gene Cate has been a career naval officer, yacht captain and has indulged in other forms of aberrent behavior from jazz disc jockey to PR executive. The Chapel Hill, NC native now resides on central Florida's east coast where, for a time, he wrote a weekly cooking column and was the restaurant critic for *Florida Today*.

He is the author of a light-hearted cookbook *"Take a Jigger of Gin..."* He swears Bubba and Z.Z. are purely figments of his imagination and are not representative of any friends and acquaintances, past or present.